'Goodnight, signora, and thank you for a lovely evening,' Salvatore said.

'Wh-what did you say?'

'I said goodnight. I think we both know the time isn't right.'

'What do you mean by that?' Helena demanded.

Salvatore spoke softly. 'I mean that when I'm ready to make love to you, I won't go to your room with the world watching.'

'*When* you— How dare you? You arrogant swine! Are you fooling yourself that I'm waiting on your pleasure?' she exclaimed.

'I'm not fooling myself, but perhaps you are. The decision has already been taken for both of us. It's only a question of when.'

Lucy Gordon cut her writing teeth on magazine journalism, interviewing many of the world's most interesting men, including Warren Beatty, Richard Chamberlain, Roger Moore, Sir Alec Guinness and Sir John Gielgud. She also camped out with lions in Africa, and had many other unusual experiences which have often provided the background for her books. She is married to a Venetian, whom she met while on holiday in Venice. They got engaged within two days.

Two of her books have won the Romance Writers of America RITA® award, SONG OF THE LORELEI in 1990, and HIS BROTHER'S CHILD in 1998, in the Best Traditional Romance category. You can visit her website at www.lucy-gordon.com

VERETTI'S DARK VENGEANCE

BY
LUCY GORDON

⊚™ MILLS & BOON®
Pure reading pleasure™

All the characters in this book have no existence outside the imagination of the author, and have no relation whatsoever to anyone bearing the same name or names. They are not even distantly inspired by any individual known or unknown to the author, and all the incidents are pure invention.

First published in Great Britain 2009
Harlequin Mills & Boon Limited,
Eton House, 18-24 Paradise Road, Richmond, Surrey TW9 1SR

© Lucy Gordon 2009

ISBN: 978 0 263 87418 1

Set in Times Roman 10½ on 11¾ pt
01-0809-51218

Printed and bound in Spain
by Litografia Rosés, S.A., Barcelona

VERETTI'S DARK VENGEANCE

CHAPTER ONE

'SHE'LL be punished for what she's done. I'm going to make sure of that if it takes me the rest of my days!'

Salvatore Veretti took one last look of loathing at the photograph in his hand before pushing back his chair and going to stand by the window overlooking the Venetian lagoon, where the morning sun was clear, brightening the deep blue sky, adding glitter to the tiny waves that laughed and curled against the boats.

He stood here every morning, relishing the beauty of Venice, bracing himself for the day ahead. There was money to be made, critics to be silenced, enemies to be defeated by one method or another. But there was also this moment of peace and beauty, and the strength it gave him.

Beauty. The thought brought his attention back to the photograph. It showed a woman, not merely lovely but physically perfect: tall, slender, exquisitely proportioned. Any man would say so, for this was a body carefully tended to please men, to be judged by men.

Salvatore, well-equipped to judge the female form, having had so many of them naked in his bed, had studied this one carefully before letting his hatred explode from him. Now he looked at it again, estimating its many beauties, and nodding as though what he saw was no more than he had expected.

But there was no softening in his coldly handsome features. If anything they grew harsher as his eyes roved over the glorious shape that was barely covered by the minute black bikini; the lush breasts, the endless legs, the shapely rear.

Calculation, he thought. Every inch carefully sculpted, every move assessed beforehand, everything planned to inflame male desire and, by that means, bring her money. And now she had the money she'd schemed to get. Or thought she had.

But I too can calculate, he mused. As you are about to discover. And when your weapons prove useless against me—what will you do then?

There was a buzz from the desk and his secretary's voice said, 'Signor Raffano is here.'

'Send him in.'

Raffano was his financial adviser and also an old friend who'd known the family through many troubles. He'd been summoned to Salvatore's office in the Palazzo Veretti to discuss urgent business. By the time he entered Salvatore had moved away from the window.

'There's more news,' Salvatore said curtly, waving the other man to a chair.

Raffano was elderly with white hair and a gentle face. In his youth he'd been flamboyant, but the passing years had left him thinner and more serious.

'You mean in addition to your cousin's death?' he enquired cautiously.

'Antonio was my father's cousin, not mine,' Salvatore reminded him. 'He was always a bit of a gadfly, likely to do stupid things without considering the consequences.'

'He was known as a man who liked to enjoy himself,' Raffano mused. 'People said it proved him a true Venetian.'

'That's a slur on all Venetians. There aren't many with his reckless disregard for everything except his own pleasures. He'd spend it, drink it or sleep with it, and to hell with the rest of the world.'

'I will admit he should have taken more responsibility for the glass factory.'

'Instead he put the whole thing in his manager's hands, and vanished into the distance, to have fun,' Salvatore said grimly.

'Probably the shrewdest thing he could have done. Emilio is a brilliant manager, and I doubt if Antonio could ever have run the place so well himself. Let's remember the best of him. He was popular and he'll be greatly missed. Will his body be coming home for burial?' Raffano asked.

'No, I gather the funeral has already taken place in Miami, where he lived these last two years,' Salvatore said. 'It is his widow who will be coming to Venice.'

'His widow?' Raffano queried. 'But was he—?'

'It seems that he was. Recently he bought the company of a flighty piece, no different from many others who had been in his life. I've no doubt he paid her well, but she wanted more. She wanted marriage so that in due course she could inherit his fortune.'

'You judge people very harshly, Salvatore. You always did.'

'And I'm right.'

'You know nothing about this woman.'

'I know *this*.' With a sharp movement Salvatore pushed the photograph over the table.

Raffano whistled as he took it. 'This is her? Are you sure? It's impossible to see her face.'

'No, it's a pity about that huge sun hat, but what does the face matter? Look at the body.'

'A body to burn a man up with desire,' Raffano agreed. 'How did you get this?'

'A mutual friend happened to bump into them a couple of

years ago. I believe they'd just met, and my friend took a quick snap and sent it to me with a note saying this was Antonio's latest "little fancy".'

'You can just see that they must have been on the beach,' Raffano said.

'The perfect setting for her,' Salvatore said wryly. 'How else could she flaunt her expensive charms? Then she whisked him off to Miami, and when she had him to herself she persuaded him to marry her.'

'When did the marriage take place?'

'I don't know. No word of it reached here, which was probably her doing. She must have known that if his family knew about the wedding they'd have put a stop to it.'

'I wonder how,' Raffano pointed out. 'Antonio was in his sixties, not a teenager to obey your orders.'

'I'd have stopped it, I promise you. There are ways.'

'Legal ways? Civilised ways?' Raffano asked, giving him a curious look.

'Effective ways,' Salvatore said with a harsh grin. 'Trust me for that.'

'To be sure. I would always trust you to do what was unscrupulous.'

'How well you know me! However, the wedding took place. It must have been at the last minute, when she saw that he was near the end and moved fast to secure an inheritance.'

'Are you sure there's been a marriage at all?'

'Yes, I've heard from her lawyers. The Signora Helena Veretti—as she now calls herself—is about to arrive and claim what she considers hers.'

The coldly sardonic edge in his voice startled even Raffano, who was used to it.

'Of course you feel bad about it,' he said. 'The factory should never have been left to Antonio in the first place. It was always understood that it was to go to your father—'

'But my father was busy getting into debt at the time and my great-aunt thought she was doing the sensible thing, leaving it to Antonio,' Salvatore supplied. 'That was all right. He was family. But this woman isn't family, and I'll be damned if I stand by and see Veretti property fall into her grasping hands.'

'It'll be hard for you to challenge the will if she's his legal wife, however recent the marriage.'

A frightening smile came over Salvatore's face.

'Don't worry,' he said. 'As you said, I know how to be unscrupulous.'

'You make it sound almost like a virtue.'

'It can be.'

'Just the same, be a little careful, Salvatore. I know you've had to be ruthless ever since you were very young, to save your family from disaster. But sometimes I wonder if you're going a little too far for your own good.'

'My own good? How can being firm possibly harm me?'

'By turning you into a tyrant, a man to be feared but never loved, and consequently a man who will end his days alone. I wouldn't say this unless I was your friend.'

Salvatore's face softened. 'I know that,' he said. 'A better friend no man ever had. But don't worry. I'm well-protected. Nothing can touch me.'

'I know. That's what worries me most.'

Everything was done. The funeral was over, the paperwork was in order, and all that was left was to check out of the hotel and head for Miami Airport.

Before starting the journey Helena went to the cemetery, to lay a final offering of flowers on her husband's grave.

'I guess this is goodbye,' she said when she'd arranged them carefully. 'I'll come back and see you again, but I don't know exactly when. It depends what I find when I get to Venice.'

A step on the path behind her made her turn far enough to see a group of people walking past, slowing so that they could see her better. She gave a faint smile.

'It's happening again,' she whispered to Antonio. 'Do you remember how we used to laugh when they stared at me?'

Her beauty had always drawn eyes, first in her years as a model then, after her retirement, the attention had continued. Her long hair was a luscious honey-colour, and her figure had remained perfect; five feet ten inches, slender but rounded.

Her face was remarkable, with large eyes and full lips that commanded attention. Those generous lips were her chief beauty for they made her smile impossible to ignore, and when held softly together they seemed to be on the verge of a kiss.

That, at least, was what one of her admirers had said. Helena had thanked him graciously, then turned away to hide her chuckles. She could never quite take her own achievements seriously, which was part of her charm. Photographers wanting to convey 'voluptuous' had always asked for her, and she was soon known in the trade as 'Helen of Troy', which made her laugh even more.

Antonio had enjoyed every moment of it.

'They look at us and say, "What a lucky fellow to have won the heart of that beautiful woman!"' he'd said with relish. 'They think what a wonderful time we must have in bed, and they envy me.'

Then he'd sighed, for the wonderful time in bed had been an illusion. His heart had been too weak to risk physical exertion, and in their two years together they had never once made love. But he'd derived much innocent pleasure from the world's speculation.

'I'm going to miss you terribly,' she told him now. 'You were wonderful to me, always so kind, giving much and taking little. With most men it's the other way around. For the first time in my life I felt loved and protected, and now suddenly I'm alone again.'

Tears streamed down her face as she touched the marble headstone.

'Why did you have to die? We always knew it was going to happen but we thought, if we were careful, we could prolong your life. And we did. You had all those extra months and things were looking good, but then suddenly...'

She could still see him as he'd been then, laughing, then stopping suddenly, his face becoming strained, laughter turning to choking as he was enveloped by his final heart attack. And it was all over.

'Goodbye,' she whispered. 'You'll always be in my heart.'

They had been so close in spirit that she felt he was still with her as the cab conveyed her to Miami Airport and she boarded the flight. In the long dark hours crossing the ocean he was there again, reminding her how their strange marriage had come about.

She'd abandoned modelling at the height of her career, tired of the life, meaning to become a businesswoman. She'd built up a healthy fortune, and only needed a way to invest it.

She'd thought herself knowledgeable, but soon discovered her mistake when a con man persuaded her to invest in a dud company. Before she'd actually signed any cheques Antonio had come to her rescue, warning her of a friend who'd been tricked in just such a way. That was how they'd met, when he saved her from disaster.

They'd become close friends. He had been in his sixties and already knew that his life could not be long. When he'd asked her to stay with him until the end she agreed without hesitation, feeling that he would ease her loneliness for whatever time they had together, as she would ease his. Their marriage ceremony had been as quiet as they could arrange and she'd tended him lovingly until the day he died in her arms.

He'd talked quite frankly about the time to come, and the provision he'd made for her, excessive provision in her opinion. She'd known he owned a glass factory on the Venetian island of Murano.

'When I'm no longer here Larezzo Glass will be yours,' he said. 'And you will go to Venice to claim it.'

'But what would I do with a glass factory?' she'd protested.

'Sell it. My relative, Salvatore, will make you a good offer.'

'How can you be so sure?'

'Because I know how badly he wants it. He wasn't pleased when it was left to me instead of him.'

'But didn't you tell me that he already has one of his own?'

'Yes, Perroni Glass is his, and they're the two best. When he owns Larezzo as well he'll dominate the whole industry. Nobody will be able to challenge him, which is just how he likes it. You can demand a high price. There's a bank loan to be paid off but there'll be enough money left after that to keep you safe. Don't refuse me, *cara*. Let me have the pleasure of knowing that I've looked after you, as you have looked after me.'

'But I don't need money,' she reminded him. 'I have plenty of my own, which you saved for me. You looked after me very effectively then.'

'Then let me look after you some more, to thank you for your care of me.'

'But we cared for each other,' she thought now. 'He showed me that all men aren't grasping and rapacious. Now he's gone and I can't see the way ahead.'

It was a long journey, first across the Atlantic to Paris, then a three-hour wait for the connecting flight to Venice. By the time she reached her destination she was nodding off. When she finally emerged from Customs she was met by an escort from the hotel. It was bliss to leave everything to him.

She had a vague awareness of the motor-boat trip across the lagoon and down the Grand Canal to the Illyria Hotel, where hands assisted her from the boat. Once in her room she nibbled at the meal that was sent up, before climbing into bed and sinking into a heavy, jet-lagged sleep.

As the hours passed her sleep became lighter and she found that Antonio was there again in her dreams, cheerful, jokey, despite his impending death, because it was his way to ignore the future as long as he could enjoy the present.

Because he flourished in hot weather they had gone to live in Miami, where they spent long, lazy days together, in contented mutual devotion. To please him she'd learned to speak Italian, and then also learned the Venetian dialect because he'd bet her she couldn't do it.

He'd tricked her about that. She'd thought it would be easy, imagining a dialect was little more than a change in pronunciation. Too late she'd discovered that Venetian was a whole different language.

Antonio had enjoyed the joke, laughing until he brought on a coughing fit and had to use his inhaler.

'Fooled you!' he gasped. 'Bet you can't do it.'

After that she had to try, and surprised herself and him by becoming good at both languages.

Antonio showed her pictures of his family, especially Salvatore, his cousin once removed, he told her, carefully stressing the 'removed', because he admired Salvatore only in a distant way, and tended to avoid him. He hadn't invited him to the wedding, or even told him about it.

'He's a hard man,' he said. 'I was always the black sheep of the family, and he disapproved of me.'

'But you're more than twenty years older than he is,' she pointed out. 'Shouldn't it be you disapproving of him?'

'I wish!' Antonio said ruefully. 'I preferred to leave running the factory to my manager, so that I could enjoy myself.'

'And Salvatore doesn't enjoy himself?'

'Well—it depends what you mean by enjoyment. Ever since he grew up he could have any woman he wanted, but they always came second to ruling the roost. He's a bit of a puritan, which is odd in a Venetian. We tend to think more about relishing life today and letting tomorrow take care of itself. But not Salvatore.

'It might be something to do with his father, my cousin, Giorgio, a man who really knew how to have a good time. Perhaps he overdid it a little with too many women. His poor wife certainly thought so. Salvatore also takes his pleasures freely, but he's more discreet, and no woman is allowed to impinge on his real life.

'Everyone's afraid of him. Even me. Venice wasn't big enough to hold both of us, so I left, travelled the world, went to England, met you, and have been happy ever since.'

Salvatore's picture showed that he was handsome, slightly fierce, with a face that was a little too firm and a mysterious air about him that Antonio told her attracted women.

'They all think they'll be the one to soften him, but none ever has. I keep meaning to take you to Venice to meet him, but I dare not.' His eyes twinkled. 'You're so beautiful he'd make a play for you in minutes.'

'Then he'd be wasting his time,' Helena had told him, laughing. 'Let's make that trip. I should like to see Venice.'

Now she was seeing Venice, but not in the way she'd hoped.

'We should have come here together,' she told Antonio, and on the words she awoke.

At first she didn't know where she was. Then she saw the high painted ceiling, elaborately decorated with cherubs, and the exotic furnishings that might have come from the eighteenth century. Slipping out of bed, she pulled on a light robe and went to the window, pushing it open to find herself bathed in dazzling light.

It was like stepping into a new universe, brilliant, magical, and she stood entranced. The water that flowed past the building was busy with boats. The landing stages were crowded with people, and everywhere she looked there was activity.

A shower brought her fully back to life, ready to go out and explore. She chose clothes that were elegant but functional, being particularly careful about the shoes.

'The stones of Venice are the hardest in the world,' Antonio had groaned. 'If you're going to walk—and you have to walk because there are no cars—don't wear high heels.'

To placate his nagging ghost she selected a pair that were flat and efficient and that looked good with hip-hugging wine-red trousers and a white blouse. Her glorious hair was swept back and fixed so that it hung down her back. Then she stood before the mirror to regard herself critically.

Neat, slightly severe, nothing that would hog attention. Good.

Having breakfast in her room would be too dull, so she went down to the restaurant to confront the banquet there.

It was one of the pleasures of her life that she could eat whatever she liked without putting on weight. Now she enjoyed herself to the full, then went to the information desk to collect some leaflets about the city. Serious business could wait while she had some fun. The young man behind the counter asked politely if she had any special reason to come to Venice.

'I'm interested in glass,' she said casually. 'I believe there are several glass factories here.'

'They are on the island of Murano, just across the water. Murano glass is the very finest in the world.'

'So I've heard. I believe there's one called Larezzo that's supposed to be the best of all.'

'Some say it is, some say that Perroni is the best. They're about equal. If you're interested in seeing a glass works there's a tour going to Larezzo today.'

'Thank you, I should like to join it.'

An hour later a large motor boat drew up by the hotel landing stage and she boarded it, along with five others. Ten tourists were already there, and the driver proclaimed that they had now made the last stop, and could head for Murano.

'Once the factories were in Venice,' Antonio had told her. 'But the city fathers were afraid of those roaring foundries, in case they started a fire that would consume the whole city. So, in the thirteenth century, they banished the glass makers to Murano.'

There they had remained ever since, dominating the art with their inventive techniques and the unrivalled beauty of their products.

Now Helena stood near the front of the boat, full of curiosity about what she would discover, and revelling in the sensation of the wind whipping about her. Of course, it made good business sense to inspect her property incognito before confronting Salvatore, but she knew, if she was honest, that she was simply enjoying this.

After fifteen minutes they arrived. Hands reached out to help them ashore, and a guide pointed out the factory.

She had never been anywhere like it before. The exhibition of finished glass objects was pleasing enough, but beyond that were the secrets of how these beautiful things were made. The furnaces, the designers, the vases being blown by hand—all these things entranced her.

She let herself fall back to the edge of the crowd, then slipped away out of sight. Now she was free to wander alone, pausing to watch as the fancy took her. It was like another universe, one where the most dazzling arts were practised with an almost casual skill.

At last she reckoned she should rejoin the others. They were just below, at the foot of the stairs, and by passing a nearby door she could reach them quietly.

The door was half-open, giving her a glimpse of a man talking into the telephone in a harsh, angry voice. She slipped past, unnoticed, and would have proceeded to the head of the stairs, had not the sound of her own name pulled her up short.

'Signora Helena Veretti, I suppose we must call her, though it goes against the grain.'

Slowly she moved backwards until she could just make him out again. He had his back to her, but suddenly he turned, giving her a glimpse of his face and making her pull back sharply.

Salvatore Veretti.

She might be mistaken. She had only an old photograph to go on.

But there was no mistake about what he was saying.

'I can't think why she's not here yet. I came to Larezzo to see if any of the staff had heard anything, but they all swear blind that there's been no sign of her.'

Now she was glad that she'd learned Venetian dialect, for without it she wouldn't have understood a word, although the ill-will in his tone was unmistakeable.

'Don't ask me what happened to the stupid woman. It doesn't really matter, except that I don't like being kept waiting.'

Really! thought Helena with wry humour.

'Whenever she arrives I'm ready for her. I know just what to expect; some smart miss on the make who married Antonio to get her hands on his money. She may have fooled him, but she won't fool me. If she thinks she's going to take over here, she's mistaken. And if she thinks I don't know the kind of woman she is, she's even more mistaken.'

There was a pause, during which Helena reckoned the other party was actually managing to get a word in edgeways. It didn't last long.

'It's no problem. She won't know what Larezzo is worth, and she'll jump at whatever I offer. If not, if she's mad enough to try to keep the place, I'll simply drive her to the wall, then buy her out for peanuts. Yes, that's fighting dirty. So what? It's the way to get results, and this is one result I'm determined to get. I'll call you later.'

Helena moved away quickly, hurrying down the stairs to rejoin the party. Now she was seething.

She'd been ready to do a reasonable deal, but this man wasn't reasonable. He wasn't even civilised. And his behaviour was beyond bearing.

If she thinks I don't know the kind of woman she is...

Those words burned into her consciousness.

I'll tell you the kind of woman I am, she mused. The kind who won't put up with your behaviour, that's for sure. The kind who'll give you a black eye and enjoy doing it. That kind.

Right! If that's how you want to play it, I enjoy a good fight.

CHAPTER TWO

HELENA slipped quietly back into the group, relieved that nobody seemed to have noticed her absence. Rico, the guide, was announcing the end of the tour.

'But before we take you back, you will please honour us by accepting some refreshment. This way please.'

He led them into a room where a long table was laid out with cakes, wine and mineral water, and began to serve them. As he was handing a glass to Helena he looked up suddenly, alerted by someone who'd just come in and was calling him in Venetian.

'Sorry to trouble you, Rico, but do you know where Emilio is?'

Helena recognised the name. Emilio Ganzi had been Antonio's trusted manager for years.

'He's out,' Rico said, 'but I'm expecting him back any moment.'

'Fine, I'll wait.'

It was him, the man she'd seen in the office, and now Helena had no doubt that this was Salvatore. She stayed discreetly back, taking the chance to study her enemy unobserved.

He bore all the signs of a worthy opponent, she had to admit that. Antonio had said he was a man who expected never to be challenged, and it was there in the set of his head, in an air of assertiveness so subtle that the unwary might fail to see it.

But she saw it, and knew exactly what Antonio had meant. Salvatore was tall, more than six foot, with black hair and eyes of a dark brown that seemed to swallow light. Helena wondered if he worked out in a gym. Beneath his conventional clothing she sensed hard muscles, proclaiming a dominance of the body as well as the mind.

His face told two different stories; one of sensuality just below the surface, one of stern self-control. He would yield nothing except for reasons of his own. Remembering the angry frustration in his voice so recently, and comparing it to the civilised ease of his manner now, she guessed that the control was in full force.

Yet, despite being masked, the sensuality asserted itself in the slight curve of his mouth, the way his lips moved against each other. There was an instinctive harmony in his whole being, a sense of power held in reserve, ready to be unleashed at any moment.

He was moving among the group, discovering that they were English and switching easily to that language, asking politely why they had wanted to visit a glass factory, and why this one in particular. His manner was friendly, his smile apparently warm. Under other circumstances Helena would have found him charming.

When he noticed her he grew still for a brief moment, which was what men always did, noticing her beauty, only half believing it. For a moment she contemplated her next move.

Why not have some fun?

Driven by an imp of wickedness, she gave him an enticing smile.

'Can I get you a glass of wine?' he asked, approaching her.

'Thank you.'

He produced it, took one himself, and walked aside with her, enquiring politely, 'Are you enjoying yourself?'

She preserved a straight face. He had no idea that she was the enemy that he was so confident of defeating. As a model she'd often needed acting skills. She used them now, assuming a note of naïve enthusiasm.

'Oh, yes, I really am. I'm fascinated by places like this. It's wonderful being able to see how things work.'

She gave him the full value of her eyes, which were large and deep blue, and had been known to make strong men weep. He rewarded her with a wry half-smile, clearly saying that he liked her looks, he wasn't fooled by her methods, but he didn't mind passing the time this way, as long as she didn't overdo it.

Cheek! she thought. He was appraising her like a potential investment, to see if it was worth his time and trouble.

Helena was as free from conceit as an accredited beauty could well be, but this was insulting. After the remarks she'd overheard it was practically a declaration of war.

But she had also declared war, although he didn't know it. Now it was time to discover the lie of the land.

'It's just a pity that the tours of this place are so short,' she sighed. 'No time to see all I wanted to.'

'Why don't I show you a little more?' he asked easily.

'That would be delightful.'

Envious looks followed her, the woman who'd captured the most attractive man in the room in two and a half minutes flat. As they departed a voice floated behind them.

'We could all do that if we had her legs.'

She gave a soft choke of laughter, and he smiled.

'I guess you're used to it,' he murmured.

He didn't add, 'A woman who looks like you.' He didn't have to.

The trip was fascinating. He was an excellent guide with a gift for explaining things simply but thoroughly.

'How do they get that wonderful ruby-red?' she marvelled.

'They use a gold solution as a colouring agent,' he told her.

Another marvel was the row of furnaces, three of them. The first contained the molten glass into which the tip of the blowpipe was dipped. When the glass had been worked on and cooled a little it was reheated in the second furnace through a hole in the door, known as the Glory Hole. This happened again and again, keeping the glass up to the ideal temperature for moulding. When the perfect shape had been achieved it went into the third furnace to be cooled slowly.

'I'm afraid you may find it uncomfortably hot in here,' Salvatore observed.

But she shook her head. True, the heat was fierce, but far from being uncomfortable it seemed to bathe her in its glow. She stood as close as she dared to the red-white light streaming from the Glory Hole, feeling as though her whole self was opening up to its fierce radiance.

'Get back,' Salvatore said, taking hold of her.

Reluctantly she let him draw her away. The heat was making her blood pound through her veins and she felt mysteriously exalted.

'Are you all right?' he asked, keeping his hands on her shoulders and looking down into her flushed face.

'Yes, I'm fine,' she murmured.

He gave her a little shake. 'Wake up.'

'I don't want to.'

He nodded. 'I know the feeling. This place is hypnotic, but you have to be careful. Come over here.'

He led her to where a man was blowing glass through a pipe, turning it slowly so that it didn't sag and lose shape. Watching him, she felt reality return.

'It's incredible that it's still done that way,' she marvelled. 'You'd think it would be easier to use a machine.'

'It is,' he said. 'There are machines that will do some kind of job, and if "some kind of job" is what you want, that's fine. But if you want a perfect job, lovingly sculpted by a glass worker who's put his soul into his art, then come to Murano.'

Something in his voice made her look at him quickly. Until now their conversation had been a light-hearted dance, but his sudden fervour made the music pause.

'There's nothing like it,' he said simply. 'In a world where things are increasingly mechanised, there's still one place that's fighting off the machines.'

Then he gave a brief, self-conscious laugh.

'We Venetians are always a little crazy about Venice. To the outside world most of what we say sounds like nonsense.'

'I don't think it's—'

'There's something else that might interest you,' he said as though he hadn't heard her. 'Shall we go this way?'

She followed him, intrigued, not by whatever he had to show her, but by the brief glimpse behind his eyes that he discouraged so swiftly.

'The glass isn't all blown,' he said, leading into the next room. 'Figurines and jewellery take just as much art of a different kind.'

One piece held her attention, a pendant in the shape of a heart. The glass seemed to be dark blue, but with every movement it changed through mauve and green. She held it in her hand, thinking of one just like it, except for the colour, safely tucked away in her jewel box in the hotel. It had been Antonio's first gift to her.

'From my heart to yours,' he'd said, smiling in a way that had moved her, because he seemed almost shy.

She'd worn it for their wedding, and again as he lay dying, just to please him.

'Do you like it?' Salvatore asked.

'It's really beautiful.'

He took it from her. 'Turn around.'

She did so, and felt him pull her long hair aside, put the chain around her neck and clasp it. His fingers barely brushed her skin but suddenly she wanted to clench her hands and take deep breaths. She wanted to take flight and run as far away from him as possible. She wanted to press closer and feel his hands on the rest of her body. She didn't know what she wanted.

Then it was over. His touch vanished. She returned to earth.

'It looks good on you,' he said. 'Keep it.'

'But this belongs to the firm. You can't give it to me, unless—oh, my goodness, you're the manager.' She put her hand over her mouth in simulated dismay. 'You are the manager, and I never realised. I've been taking up your time—'

'No, I'm not the manager.'

'Then you're the owner?'

The question seemed to disconcert him. He didn't reply and she pushed her advantage.

'You do own this place, don't you?'

'Yes,' he said. 'At least, I will soon, when some trivial formalities are cleared up.'

Helena stared at him. This was arrogance on a grand scale.

'Trivial formalities,' she echoed. 'Oh, I see. You mean the sale is agreed and you'll take over in a few days. How wonderful!'

He made a wry face.

'Not quite as fast as that. Sometimes things take a little negotiating.'

'Aw, c'mon, you're kidding me. I bet you're one of those— what do they call them?—speculators. Yc see, you want, you're sure to get. But someone's being a vkward about it, right?'

To her surprise he grinned.

'Maybe a little,' he conceded. 'But nothing I can't cope with.'

It was marvellous, she thought, how amusement transformed his face, giving it a touch of charm.

'What about the poor owner?' she teased. 'Does he know it's "in hand," or is that delightful surprise waiting for him as he steps around a dark corner?'

This time he laughed outright.

'I'm not a monster, whatever you may think. No dark corners, I swear it. And the owner is a woman who probably has a few tricks of her own.'

'Which, of course, you'll know how to deal with.'

'Let's just say that I've never been bested yet.'

'There's a first time for everything.'

'You think so?'

Helena regarded him with her head on one side, her eyes challenging and provoking.

'I know your kind,' she said. 'You think you can "cope with" anything because you've never learned different. You're the sort of man who makes other people long to sock you on the jaw, just to give you a new experience.'

'I'm always open to new experiences,' he said. 'Would you like to sock me on the jaw?'

'One day I'm sure I will,' she said in a considering voice. 'Just now it would be too much effort.'

He laughed again, a disconcertingly pleasant sound, with a rich vibrancy that went through her almost physically.

'Shall we store it up for the future?' he asked.

'I'll look forward to that,' she said, meaning it.

'Do you challenge every man you meet?'

'Only the ones I think need it.'

'I could make the obvious answer to that, but let's have a trucc instead.'

'As long as it's armed,' she reminded him.

'My truces are always armed.'

He stopped a passing young woman and spoke to her in Venetian. When she'd departed he said,

'I asked her to bring us some refreshment outside, where we can sit down.'

Outside was a wooden seat on a terrace that overlooked a small canal with shops along the bank. It was pleasant to sit there drinking coffee.

'Is this your first visit to Venice?' he asked.

'Yes, I've thought about it for years but never got around to it before.'

'Do you travel alone?'

'Quite alone.'

'I find that hard to believe.'

'I wonder why.'

'Let us not play games. You don't need me to say that a woman as beautiful as you need never lack company.'

'But perhaps you need to hear that a woman may prefer to be alone. It isn't always the man's choice, you know. Sometimes she consults her own preferences and consigns men to the devil.'

He gave a wry smile. '*Touché!* I suppose I asked for that.'

'You certainly did.'

'And have you consigned us all to the devil?'

'Some of you. There are men who are fit for nothing else.'

He nodded. 'You must have met quite a few of them.'

'A fair number. The virtues of solitude can be very appealing.'

'And so you travel alone,' he said slowly.

'Alone—but not lonely.'

That seemed to disconcert him. After a moment he said quietly, 'Then you must be the only person who isn't.'

'To be enough for yourself,' she answered, 'safe from the onslaughts of other people, and happy to be so—it isn't really very hard.'

'That's not true, and you know it,' he replied, looking at

her intently. 'If you've achieved it, you're one in a million. But I don't believe that you have achieved it. It's your way of fooling the world—or yourself.'

She felt as if a hand had been laid on her shoulder, halting her in her tracks. It was a moment before she drew a deep breath and said, 'I don't know if you're right. Perhaps I never will.'

'But *I* would like to know,' he said in the same quiet tone. 'I'd like to see behind that mask you keep so firmly in place.'

'If I removed it for everyone, there would be no point in having it,' she pointed out.

'Not everyone. Just me.'

Suddenly she found it hard to breathe. It was as though a cloud had crossed the sun, throwing the world into shadow, making complex things that had seemed simple only a moment before.

'Why should I tell you what I tell nobody else?' she managed to say at last.

'Only you can decide that.'

'That's true. And my decision is...' She hesitated. Something in his eyes was trying to make her say what he wanted to hear, but it had to be resisted. 'My decision is that I've kept my secrets safe so far, and I'll go on doing just that.'

'You think your secrets are safe, do you?'

Something in his voice filled her with the conviction that nothing in the world was safe, her secrets, her heart, herself—nothing.

'I think—I think I shall work hard to keep them safe.'

'And woe betide intruders?'

'Exactly.'

'But don't you know that your attitude is, in itself, a challenge to intruders?'

She smiled. She was beginning to feel at ease again.

'Of course I know. But I've fought this battle before, and I always win.'

He raised her hand and brushed the back of it with his lips. She took a long, shaky breath.

'So do I,' he assured her.

'Do you know, that's twice you've told me you're invincible, once about business and once about—well, whatever?'

'Why don't you give it a name?' he asked.

She met his eyes. 'Perhaps names don't matter.'

Before he could reply her attention was caught by the sound of a motor. Turning her head, she just made out the boat that had brought her here, appearing around the edge of the building and streaking away across the water.

'Hey, they should have waited for me,' she protested.

'I told them not to. I said I'd take you back myself.'

'You told them to go without me?' she said slowly. 'Without asking me first?'

'I was sure that you would agree with me.'

'No you weren't. That's why you didn't tell me. You've got a cheek!'

'In that case I apologise. I meant no harm.'

'Of course not,' she said affably. 'Just to get your own way with the least inconvenience. Where's the harm in that?'

'I couldn't agree more.'

'I suppose the poor idiot who owns this place is going to get the same treatment until she gives in.'

'Don't pity her; she's no idiot but a very clever woman who got her hands on Larezzo by cunning and will sell it for the highest price she can extort.'

'And since you want the place, she's laughing.'

'I doubt she'll be laughing when I've finished. Let's not talk about her further. She isn't interesting and you still haven't told me your name.'

She was saved from having to answer by the sight of Rico appearing behind him.

'I think you're wanted,' she said.

Rico was anxious to let him know that the manager had now returned and awaited his pleasure. Salvatore thanked him and turned back to Helena.

She was gone.

'What the—? Did you see where she went?'

'Round that corner, *signor*,' Rico said.

But when Salvatore followed he found himself facing a small piazza with no less than four exits and nothing to show which one she had taken. He made a token pursuit, hurrying from one little street to another, peering vainly down the narrow length of each, but knowing it was useless.

At last he stopped, furious at how easily she'd given him the slip on his own territory. Before returning he adjusted his expression so that he could say casually to Rico,

'Do you happen to know who she was?'

'No, *signor*. She just came as one of the group. Is it important?'

'No, not important at all,' he said heartily. 'Let's get back to business.'

Helena found that it was simple to return to Venice. Taxis were as easy to come by as in any other city, except that they moved on water. Soon she was streaking back across the lagoon, trying to sort out her conflicting emotions.

Satisfaction warred with annoyance. She'd bearded the enemy in his lair, looked him over, assessed him, been intrigued by him, and come off best in their parting. All that remained now was to make him suffer for his cheap opinion of her.

And she knew just the way.

Antonio had told her about the Venice grapevine.

'Whisper a secret at one end of the Grand Canal and it'll reach the other end before you do,' he'd said.

Now she put it to the test.

Returning to the Illyria, she headed back to the information desk, where the same young man was still on duty.

'I've had the most wonderful day,' she enthused. 'Isn't Venice just the loveliest city? And to think I own a little part of it!'

She bubbled on, making sure that he knew she was the widow of Antonio Veretti and the new owner of Larezzo Glass. He understood precisely, as she could tell from the way his eyes were popping. As she danced into the elevator she was sure he was reaching for the telephone.

In her room she settled down to make enjoyable decisions. This dress? No, too blatant. That one, then—black, elegant, slightly severe. But she didn't know when their meeting would occur. It might be daytime, so perhaps something more businesslike would be suitable. In the end she laid out several outfits, ready for her final decision.

As she got out of the shower the telephone rang. She answered cautiously, meaning to disguise her voice, but the man at the other end wasn't Salvatore.

'Am I talking to Signora Helena Veretti?'

'You are.'

'I am secretary to Signor Salvatore Veretti. He asks me to say that he was very glad to hear of your arrival in Venice, and looks forward to a meeting.'

Helena assumed her most formal voice to say,

'How kind of Signor Veretti.'

'Would this evening be too soon?'

'Not at all.'

'He suggests dinner at the Palazzo Veretti. His boatman will call for you at seven-thirty.'

'I look forward to it.'

She hung up, and sat still for a moment, caught off-guard by something happening inside her.

The invitation was exactly what she'd wanted, so it was

illogical that she was assailed by doubt, but she had the sudden shocking feeling of confusion. It made no sense, she told herself. She had nothing to fear from this man. The power was in her hands, not his.

Hands. The word seemed to leap out at her. His hands on the nape of her neck, caressing fingers touching, retreating, touching again. And herself trying to breathe through the storm that had engulfed her without warning.

Never, never again! She'd promised herself that long ago as a child of sixteen, when the brutal end to her first love had left her hostile to men and frozen to their caresses.

They didn't know. Stupid as they were, there wasn't one of them who could see past the façade of sexual availability that had been her trademark, to the bleak, icy truth within. She'd played them off against each other, used them to climb to the pinnacle of her career, made money out of them. And she'd slept alone.

In all those years she'd never again known the dizzying, irresistible desire that had once carried her to disaster. Once or twice a faint whisper of pleasure had troubled her but she'd controlled it, fleeing the man, never letting him suspect. With time, those occasions had grown rarer.

Looking down the vista of her future life, she'd been prepared for loneliness. Instead she'd found Antonio, a man who'd adored her without being able to risk a physical relationship. They had been perfect for each other. And his true legacy wasn't wealth, but the fact that he'd made her strong, strong enough to face an uncertain future.

'Hell!' she thought, exasperated with herself. 'I'm thirty-two. Next stop, middle-age. I've managed so far. I can manage the rest.'

So, the black dress, one of Antonio's last gifts to her, chosen for its allure. It was silk, tight-fitting, with a neckline that dropped just a little. The hem came to just above her knees, not high enough for immodesty, but high enough to show off her long legs. And after a day in sensible shoes it was a pleasure to don high heels.

She let her luxuriant hair hang loose, not drawn back as during the day, but free-flowing over her shoulders.

Her jewellery was restrained. Apart from her wedding ring she wore only a dainty gold watch, two tiny diamond studs in her ears and Antonio's glass heart. Unlike the blue shading of Salvatore's gift, this one was dark red, sometimes lightening to deep pink, but always returning to a hue that was like red roses.

'Right,' she told the mirror. 'Let battle commence.'

CHAPTER THREE

SHE waited downstairs, and at last the doorman came to escort her out to the waiting boat, which turned out to be a gondola. The gondolier bowed as he handed her in, saw her comfortably settled and moved off.

Early evening was the best time to see the Grand Canal. Lights blazed from the windows of the buildings lining the banks, and the April sun was setting, casting a glow on the water with its throng of boats. At this time of day they were mostly gondolas, conveying tourists to dinner, sightseeing, music, romance. The air was alive with the anticipation of pleasure.

'Is it very far?' she called up and over her shoulder to where the gondolier was standing behind her, plying his single oar.

'Very little distance, *signora*. The Palazzo Veretti is further along the Grand Canal. It is magnificent. Everyone admires it.'

A moment later she saw what he meant as they turned the canal's curve and the building came into sight. It was, as he'd said, magnificent, pale grey marble, ornately decorated in the Renaissance style, rising four storeys, each with ten windows facing the canal, all lit up.

She drew an admiring breath at its beauty, at the same time noting the message of dominance that came from every line.

This was the home of a man who was powerful, and wanted everyone to know it.

The gondola was turning, heading for the landing stage at the front of the *palazzo*. And there, standing in readiness, his eyes fixed on her approach, was Salvatore.

She watched his face and saw that in the evening light he wasn't quite sure what he was seeing. As the gondola drew up to the landing stage he reached out to help her from the boat. She felt the strong clasp of his hand, drawing her up until they were level. His hand tightened as he saw her face, but there was a shadow of doubt in his eyes. Was she? Wasn't she?

She gave him a deliberately challenging smile, full of amusement at his expense, calculated to annoy him.

'Good evening, Signor Valetti,' she said sweetly. 'How kind of you to invite me here tonight.'

'You?' he said slowly. 'Did I invite—you?'

'You invited Signora Helena Veretti,' she said, 'and I am she. I hope I don't come as a disappointment.'

His eyes narrowed.

'Not a disappointment, *signora*. A surprise perhaps.'

'You mean a shock, don't you?'

'Perhaps I do,' he said slowly.

'Ah, that little trick I played on you this afternoon. Was it very bad of me? Are you angry?'

'Of course not. I hope I can appreciate a joke as well as the next man.'

He was lying, Helena knew. His smiling civility was for the boatman's benefit. Beneath it he was furious at being wrong-footed.

Good!

He paid the gondolier, who seemed pleasantly surprised by the amount, and made himself scarce.

Offering her his arm, Salvatore led her into the brightly lit

. downstairs hall, with its sweeping staircase. Only then did he look at her closely enough to see what she was wearing around her neck. He drew a sharp breath as he saw the glass heart, so like the one he'd given her that afternoon, but deep red.

'A gift from my husband,' she said, touching it.

'I congratulate you, *signora,* a very clever performance. No wonder you wouldn't tell me your name.'

'It would have been a pity to spoil a good joke.'

'It would indeed. But let us leave that matter for later. I've brought you here to enjoy the very best meal of your life.'

You've brought me here to crush me, she thought, amused. *Now you need a delay to regroup your forces.*

He led her into a large room, ornately furnished with items that seemed several hundred years old. In her first confused impression she could only tell that everything here was costly.

Antonio had told her the history of the *palazzo,* which had once belonged to a noble family called Cellini.

'But they spent all their money about a hundred years ago. Then along came the upstart Verettis, with no title but plenty of money, and bought them out at a rock-bottom price— which is how they always prefer to buy. Remember that when you're negotiating with Salvatore.'

Oh, yes, she thought. *I'll remember.*

Salvatore showed her to a sofa and turned to the drinks table.

'I think I can offer you something a little better than this afternoon,' he said.

'But this afternoon you were only a surrogate host for the real owner,' she reminded him gaily.

'How true,' he said, refusing to rise to the bait. 'I suppose I owe you an apology.'

'Don't apologise. I've never been so entertained in my life.'

She saw a flash of real anger in his glance, suppressed so

quickly that anyone less alive to his reactions might have missed it. It was dangerous to taunt him, but that only made it all the more exciting.

The wine was excellent, almost a statement of superiority in itself. She sipped it slowly for a brief moment, then set it down.

'A little more?' he asked.

'No, thank you. I'm keeping my wits about me tonight.'

'In that case, why don't we eat?'

He led her to a table by a tall window that opened onto a balcony looking down onto the Grand Canal, and politely held out a seat for her.

At first the Venetian cuisine held her silent, being too delicious to interrupt. But at last she glanced up, smiling, to say,

'This really is the best food of my life, just as you said.'

'Signora—'

'Why don't you just call me Helena? Surely we're already beyond the need for formalities?'

'I agree. Helena—'

'I expect we're ready to get down to business now. We've both had time to get our thoughts in order.'

'Ah, business. You're right. Name the price.'

She stared.

'Did I hear right? You dare say that to me—after everything I heard you say today?'

'You tricked me.'

'Just as well, or I wouldn't have known what you were really thinking.'

'You were enjoying yourself, weren't you?' he accused.

'Well, can you blame me? You were so certain you could make me dance to your tune that you were an irresistible target.'

He made a wry face, conceding her point.

'Perhaps I was a little incautious,' he agreed. 'I naturally assumed that you'd be glad to sell for the best price you could get.'

'Why naturally? Perhaps I want to stay and enjoy my husband's legacy.'

He made a sound of impatience. 'Please, let's not have that pretence.'

'Ah, yes, of course, you're so sure you know the truth about me.' She began to quote, speaking in the Venetian she'd heard him use earlier that day. '"Some smart miss on the make who married Antonio just before he died, to get her hands on his money. She may have fooled him, but she won't fool me."'

'*What?*'

'"If she thinks she's going to take over here, she's mistaken,"' Helena continued quoting. '"And if she thinks I don't know *the kind of woman she is,* she's even more mistaken."'

She waited for him to reply but he only watched her with eyes as hard as stone.

'I went to the factory in all innocence,' she continued. 'I just wanted to see it after Antonio had told me so much. It was sheer chance I happened to pass the office while you were on the phone. I'm glad I did. When somebody has a cruel and insulting opinion of you, it's always best to know.'

Salvatore rose sharply and strode away from the table as though he couldn't bear to be near her. Turning, he stared as though he'd just seen her for the first time, and didn't like it.

'You—speak—Venetian?' he said slowly.

'Antonio taught me. He bet me that I couldn't learn that as well as Italian. And there's something else you'd better get straight. Here.'

Opening her bag, she took out a paper and held it out to him. It was her marriage certificate.

'Look at the date,' she said. 'If Antonio had lived a little longer we'd have celebrated our second anniversary. I did not marry him "at the last minute".'

She had the satisfaction of seeing him redden.

'And nor do I need his money,' she finished. 'I didn't marry him for money and I don't need a quick sale now. Please understand that.'

'All right.' He held up his hands. 'We got off on the wrong foot—'

'No, *you* got off on the wrong foot, jumping to conclusions about me and spreading inaccurate rumours all over Venice. I could probably sue you for slander.'

'Have you finished?'

'No, I've barely started.'

'Suppose I don't want to listen?'

'Did I ask what you want?' Helena saw his surprise and moved in for the kill. 'It isn't nice being bullied, is it? Not that I suppose I do it as well as you, but give me a little time to practise.'

'And I'm sure you'll take every opportunity,' he observed, regarding her ironically.

'Do you blame me?'

'Not at all. In your position I should do exactly the same. Always kick the enemy when he's down. It's the most efficient way.'

'So you don't deny that you're my enemy?' she said.

'I'd look rather foolish denying it now, wouldn't I? Why expose myself to your derision by trying?'

Before she could reply the door opened and the maid appeared with the next course. He returned to the table and they both remained silent until they were alone again.

'I could always apologise,' Salvatore said carefully.

'For everything?'

'Everything I can remember. If I forget anything I dare say you'll remind me.'

'I can forgive everything except that last remark—"the kind of woman she is". What kind of woman am I, Salvatore?'

'Please—do we have to go into that?'

'I think we do. Surely you're not asking me to spare your blushes. Or is it mine you're trying to spare? "A smart miss on the make—married him for his money." Why don't you just call me a prostitute and have done with it?'

She had the pleasure of seeing that her frankness made him uneasy.

'Let's say instead a very clever lady,' he said.

'No, let's say prostitute because that's what you meant. Have the courage of your convictions. If you're going to call me names, do it to my face.'

'You're right, *signora,* I don't like being bullied—'

'No, you prefer doing the bullying.'

'Silenzio!' he snapped in a voice like a whip crack. 'If you don't mind I'd like to speak without being interrupted and without having words put into my mouth. I did not call you a prostitute—'

'It was what you meant.'

'Kindly don't tell me what I mean. *I* will tell *you* what I mean. If you were married to Antonio for two years then I must respect that, but it doesn't change my opinion that you saw a good thing and secured it for yourself. Why else does a young and beautiful woman marry a man in his sixties?'

'There are a dozen reasons, none of which you would understand.'

'To be sure, anyone who doesn't see the matter through your eyes is an ignorant buffoon—'

'Your words—'

'But you know the truth about yourself, although for some reason you pretend not to. If I say you're beautiful I'm not paying you a compliment. Beauty like yours is a trap, a menace. You see it every time you look in the mirror and work to bring it to perfection so that your snares are laid and your victims are helpless.'

'And you think Antonio was my victim?'

'No doubt of it. He was a lover of beauty, and an even greater lover of sexual allure. You must have found him easy prey. Did you look for him the way you look now?'

'Yes, he liked me this way. The more I flaunted myself before other men the more he enjoyed it, because it made them jealous of him.'

'And did he also tell you to go on flaunting yourself when he was dead?' Salvatore demanded ironically.

'Oddly enough he did. He actually bought me this dress and ordered me to wear it because he said, "Don't you dare hide yourself behind widow's weeds. I want the world to see you as I knew you." You were wondering why a widow of only a few weeks dresses in this fashion, well, now you know. I'm obeying my husband's command.'

He was about to make a sound of disbelief when it came to him that this was exactly the kind of thing Antonio would have said. The old reprobate had a way of coming out with things no other man would have said.

'I wonder why you obey this particular command right now,' he mused. 'Am I supposed to become a helpless victim?'

'You don't seem very helpless to me,' she remarked.

'That's because I'm protected. I know *women like you*. I know how you think, and calculate, what you want and how you go about getting it. You don't even try to hide it, I'll give you that.'

'You flatter yourself if you think I'm trying to add your scalp to my collection. Why would I want to do that?' Helena asked incredulously.

'Because I'm an enemy, of course. What could be more satisfying? Since you prefer honesty, let's be honest. Subdue the enemy first, then make your demands.'

His voice was cold and dangerous. Recklessly she upped the ante.

'And just what do you think I want from you, Salvatore? I hold all the cards, which means I make the terms. I don't even need to "subdue" you, the way you imply.'

He drew a sharp breath. 'You're a very courageous woman.'

'No, I'm not. I'm just the woman who's got something *you* want and isn't going to meekly hand it over. Why would I need courage for that?'

'For several reasons that I can think of but you probably can't. You're a stranger here. You should ask around. There are many who will tell you that I always get what I want, because my methods are—irresistible.'

'I'm shaking in my shoes—I don't think.' In a deliberately provocative voice she added, 'If I don't choose to sell there isn't a thing you can do about it.'

'There's a great deal I can do about it.'

'Oh, yes, now I remember! You were going to drive me to the wall and buy me out for peanuts. How could I possibly have forgotten that? Probably because I was in a fit of laughter.'

His face darkened as though he was containing his fury with difficulty, but she was on a high, and nothing would make her stop now.

'And don't count on me not knowing what Larezzo is worth,' she went on. 'You've told me what a powerful man you are in Venice, but powerful men have enemies. I'll bet there are a dozen people willing—no, eager to tell me about the value, and give me tips on your weaknesses.'

He was on his feet, looking down into her eyes.

'So you think you can find my weaknesses?' he said.

She moved a little closer so that her breath brushed his face.

'I think I've found one now,' she whispered.

He took hold of her arms and she knew at once that she was right. He was trembling. How far, she wondered, did she dare push him? Just a little further?

But she was thwarted by the sound of footsteps, and broke away from him just as the door opened. It was the maid.

'Signor Raffano is on the telephone.'

Salvatore was pale, but his voice was calm. 'I'm just coming.' To Helena he said, 'Will you excuse me a moment? I must just deal with this.'

'Of course.'

In the next room Salvatore picked up the phone. *'Pronto!'*

'I just had to find out how you were doing,' came Raffano's voice. 'Have you set the price yet?'

'No, this is going to take time.'

'Difficult, is she?'

'Let's just say she's not what I expected.'

'What does that mean?'

Salvatore ground his teeth. 'It means that she wrong-footed me.'

'Heaven help her!'

'It might be heaven help *me,*' Salvatore admitted reluctantly. 'This is one very clever lady. I made the mistake of underestimating her.' In a reflective voice he added, 'Which I won't do again.'

Left alone, Helena began to explore the room, which, at one end, became a picture gallery, and she walked slowly along the portraits. Many were of the Cellini family, as the notes beneath them proclaimed. But the last ones were Valettis, stern-faced makers of money in the nineteenth century.

More recently the pictures weren't paintings but large photographs, one of which made her pause and regard it fondly.

There was Antonio, years before she'd met him, probably in his late thirties, before his hair had turned from black to grey and started to fall out. She'd known him as a ruin, but once he'd been this fine young cavalier. Some of his wickedly handsome looks had remained to the end, and she could still see the Antonio she'd known.

Salvatore, coming to find her, found her standing before Antonio's picture, so lost in it that she didn't hear him. From this angle he could just make out the fond look on her face, the tenderness of her smile. As he watched she raised her fingers to her lips and blew a kiss. She might, or might not, have given a little sigh. He couldn't be sure.

Helena seemed to become aware of him.

'Look at his eyes,' she said, indicating the picture. 'He was a real devil, wasn't he?'

'He was in his youth. What about when you knew him?'

'We—ell,' she mused, remembering Antonio's frailty, and thinking that a man didn't have to be physically capable to be a devil. There were other ways, charming ways that ended in laughter. Remembering those times, she smiled, her eyes fixed on the distance.

Salvatore, watching intently, saw what he'd expected. She had seduced Antonio into action, driving him beyond his strength until he reached the inevitable end. Suddenly he was angry with himself for forgetting so easily that she was an experienced temptress. Her smile, with its hint of a secret history, told him everything he needed to know.

It was a useful reminder not to forget again.

She passed on and he stood for a moment, considering the soft seductiveness of her walk, the way one part of her body moved against another, which could drive a man to distraction.

Or to death, he thought.

He caught up with her as she paused before a wedding picture.

'My parents,' he said.

It was the bride who held Helena's attention; young, beautiful, glowing with joy and love, she couldn't tear her gaze from her groom. The man was clearly Salvatore's father, yet there was something missing. His features were similar, but he lacked the driven intensity of his son, an intensity that would always make Salvatore stand out in the world.

Near-by was a picture that showed more of the family. There was Salvatore, seemingly in his early teens, surrounded by older people, presumably aunts and uncles.

'And there's Antonio,' she said, peering. 'Who's the woman sitting beside him?'

'That's my mother.'

'*What?* But she—?'

Astounded, Helena stared, trying to believe that this middle-aged woman was the same person as the glorious bride of the earlier picture. She was too thin, her whole aspect was tense and strained, and Helena had the feeling that she was putting on a brave, defiant face for the world. She stood just behind the young Salvatore, her glance turned slightly towards him, her hand possessively on his shoulder, as though he was all she had.

She looked back and forth between the two pictures, horrified.

'How did it happen?' she asked. 'She's so changed.'

'People do change with the passing of time,' he observed.

'But it can't have been many years after the wedding, and she looks as though some dreadful tragedy had happened to her.'

'My mother took her duties very seriously, not only in the home but also in the many charities she supported.'

He spoke in a distant voice that made Helena feel he was warning her off the subject. She was dissatisfied. There was more here than simply passing years. Yet she supposed she had no right to ask further. She took one last look at the picture.

'Poor woman,' she sighed. 'How sad she seems!'

Salvatore didn't answer, and she guessed he was offended by her continued interest. But when she glanced at his face she saw it strangely softened.

'Yes,' he said quietly. 'She was. Shall we go back?'

It was almost a surprise to discover that there was still food on the table from their abandoned meal. So much had happened since, not outwardly but inwardly. They had confronted each other from behind carefully erected barriers of mistrust and dislike, but neither had allowed for the random chance of physical attraction.

It defied belief. It was unexpected, unwanted, but undeniable. As malign and frisky as a jester, it danced between them, laughing at them both, caught in its trap.

Helena had no doubt that he was as trapped as herself. She knew it, not through vanity, but through her senses, fiercely alive as they hadn't been for years, not since— She shut the thought off there.

Her mind swung obediently into action. Stay cool. Stay in charge.

She sat down, aiming a smile at him like a missile.

'Now I must finish this cake. It's delicious.'

'Some coffee?'

'How delightful!'

They were back behind their defences, looking out, keeping watch, big guns primed, ready for anything.

'So,' he said at last, 'you're going to make me wait for the factory?'

'At the very least. At the most you won't get it at all.'

'You're not seriously planning to keep it?' he demanded in a tone of incredulity that riled her.

'Isn't that what I've been saying all this time? Or weren't you listening?'

'I didn't take it seriously. You were annoyed with me, perhaps rightly so, but you've had your fun and now it's time to get real.'

'You're right. So listen to me. I *really* don't intend to sell. Why should I?'

'Because you know nothing about it,' he said, exasperated. 'No woman genuinely understands business.'

'I don't believe I heard that. Come into the twenty-first century.'

'If you're planning to run that place, be my guest. You'll be bankrupt in no time and fall into my hands.'

'Of course I'm not going to run it personally. Antonio told me that the manager is excellent. Don't count on forcing me to sell. You can't.'

'I think you'll find I can. I have a number of aces up my sleeve.'

'I'm sure of it, but I have a few myself.'

Unexpectedly he smiled, raising his glass in salute.

'Here's to our confrontation,' he said. 'Let's hope we both enjoy it equally.'

'Oh, I mean to,' she said, toasting him.

He began to laugh, surprising her with a tone that sounded genuinely warm, even charming. But that was just another of his tricks, she reminded herself quickly.

'We've travelled a long, winding journey tonight,' he said. 'Have two people ever learned so much about each other in such a short time, yet still known nothing at all?'

'Nothing at all,' she echoed. 'Yes, we'd both be wise to remember that, wouldn't we?'

'If it's possible, but the danger with illusions is that they seem so much like reality—at least, that's true of the best of them, the most desirable.'

She nodded. 'Then we enter a conspiracy against our-selves,' she murmured, 'believing what we wish to believe, persuading ourselves that illusion is reality and reality illusion. And how do we ever know?'

'That's easy,' he said wryly. 'We know when it's too late.'

'Yes,' she whispered. 'That's true.'

Salvatore was about to reply but something he saw in her eyes held him silent. She was looking into the distance and he had the feeling that she no longer saw him, or even knew that he was there.

'What is it?' he said urgently. 'Helena, speak to me.'

But she was silent, lost in a world he couldn't enter.

CHAPTER FOUR

HELENA was in another place, one in which the air sang with a hundred new impressions. The most disconcerting was the way she and Salvatore were talking, as though there was an instinctive connection between their thoughts. It was surely impossible, yet he knew what she was thinking, in a way that had only ever been true with Antonio.

It wouldn't last. They were still enemies, but for a shocking moment she could see ahead to another world where enemies clung together in uneasy alliance.

Then the mist cleared and the world settled back into its right place.

'It's time I was leaving,' she said slowly. 'Will you summon your gondolier?'

'If you wish, but I should prefer to walk you back to the hotel.'

'All right. Thank you.'

He fetched her wrap and laid it gently about her shoulders. She drew breath, bracing herself for the feel of his fingers on her skin, but it didn't come. Accidentally or by design he'd contrived to drape the silk without touching her.

She shivered.

They left the building by a side door which led directly into a tiny alley that she knew was called a *calle,* so narrow that she could have touched both sides at once. The buildings rose up high, so that it was almost like being in a tunnel. She leaned back, gazing up into the narrow strip of sky, so fascinated that she began to walk on without seeing where she was going, and Salvatore had to grasp her quickly.

'You nearly walked into a door,' he said.

'Where are we?' she murmured. 'I'm lost.'

'It isn't far back to the hotel. You came around the long curve in the canal, but we'll cut across that. Didn't Antonio tell you how deceptive distances can be in Venice?'

He still had one arm around her shoulder, guiding her, so that she could look up as she walked, and still feel safe.

'He didn't tell me everything,' she said.

'I'm glad of that. I'm so glad.' After a moment he asked, 'What did he tell you about me?'

She laughed, a soft sound deep in her throat, that briefly made his hand tighten.

'He said I should beware,' she said.

'And will you?'

'I always trusted Antonio's advice, and it was always good.'

'Probably wise. Did he tell you that you're strong enough to challenge me, or did you discover that for yourself?'

'I knew in the first moment.'

He turned her towards him, looking down into her face, illuminated by the moonlight. His own face was in shadow, but she could see his eyes and read their meaning.

'Because you knew your weapons were the best,' he murmured. 'And just now, I'm ready to admit that. I'm not even trying to resist them because they overcome me, so that I don't even want to resist.'

She felt his hands on the side of her face, saw his head block out the moon so that there was only darkness as his lips touched hers. And she was glad of the darkness because suddenly everything changed, the world was a different place and nothing was as it had been.

His mouth was gentle, moving with leisurely ease as though he had all the time in the world. Helena held her breath, transfixed by something that was happening deep inside her in an unknown region. She'd guessed this was coming, had thought herself ready, but nothing could have prepared her for the way she was coming alive.

It was as though no life had ever existed before. The world had begun that moment and it was a glorious place, full of light and fire. With all her being she wanted to explore further, to see how intense the heat might become, how blinding the light.

He'd spoken of being overcome by her, yet it was she who was being overcome, not by force but by temptation so strong that it destroyed her will. She put up her hands to his shoulders, perhaps meaning to push him away but actually holding on to him.

Years of abstinence had taught her to think of herself as a cold woman, whose fire had flamed briefly and then died forever. So many men had reached this point and she'd kissed them, hoping to fan the flame back to life, but it had never happened. Dead. Cold and dead.

Until now, with this one man who should have been the very last to attract her. They were combatants, hostile, determined to think the worst of each other because it was safer that way. But in his arms there was no safety, nor did she want any. Enmity, she discovered, could be thrilling.

So she drew him closer and moved her lips against his, seeking more of the pleasure that had come like a bolt from the blue. Feeling her response, he responded in turn, letting his hands explore her, but so lightly that at first she wasn't sure it was happening. But then there was no doubt. His caresses had the skill of the devil, touching, inciting, then moving on, leaving a trail of excitement behind them.

Now she wanted him, wanted everything with him. She

must take him to her bed, lie with him naked, offer herself to him and claim him inside her at the same moment. And when he entered her she would keep him there, for pleasure such as this could not be rushed.

Instinct told her that he could show her new worlds, carry her to the stars and satisfy something desperate inside her that had been denied too long. All her frustrated womanhood rose up, crying out for release, ready to do anything, offer him anything if he would only take her to that peak.

Offer him anything!

The words seemed to shriek, like demons howling with laughter at her naïvety. How easily he'd brought her to this moment, and she, who'd prided herself on being armed and ready, had succumbed without a protest. How he must be enjoying it!

It was over. The desire, so tormenting one minute, was extinguished the next, turning her body to ice. Part of her wanted to cry out as the beauty vanished, but another part knew that she was safer this way.

Safety. That was what mattered. Nothing else.

Vaguely she heard footsteps, felt his arms loosen about her, heard his sigh of resignation.

'People are coming,' he growled. 'We don't want to be stared at.'

He drew her away and in a few moments they had reached St. Mark's Square. Not much further to the hotel, and as she walked she was planning what to say when they got there.

How sure of himself he must be. How easily she'd fallen for it. How he must be laughing in triumph, and how she was going to enjoy wiping the smile off his face!

They were entering the hotel. She would let him escort her to the elevator, shake hands and coolly bid him goodbye. Just a few more feet. There was the elevator, the doors were opening—

'I'll leave you here,' he said. 'Goodnight, *signora,* and thank you for a lovely evening.'

'Wh—what did you say?'

'I said goodnight. I think we both know the time isn't right.'

'What do you mean by that?' Helena demanded.

Salvatore spoke softly.

'I mean that when I'm ready to make love to you, I won't go to your room with the world watching.'

'*When* you— How dare you? You arrogant swine! Are you fooling yourself that I'm waiting on your pleasure?' she exclaimed.

'I'm not fooling myself, but perhaps you are. The decision has already been taken for both of us. It's only a question of when. That was clear to both of us from the first moment.'

'I know no such—'

'Don't pretend,' he cut her off harshly. 'You know as well as I do what lies ahead. You decided to seduce me in the exact same moment you became my enemy, as a demonstration of power. That's fine because I decided the same thing, and when the time comes the power will be equal. I may even allow you to see how badly I want you, but I'll do it at a time and a place of my own choosing. Is that clear?'

'You must be out of your mind,' Helena said furiously.

'No, but I have seen into yours, and I find it fascinating. Let us not rush. We can fight and fight, and please each other at the same time. I look forward to it.'

'Well, I certainly don't.'

She stormed into the elevator and tried to close the door against him, but he moved quickly to get in beside her, closing the doors and pressing a button that held them closed.

'You're lying, Helena,' he said. 'Or perhaps you're just deceiving yourself. Whichever it is, we'll both enjoy finding out.'

'We will not. Kindly get out, *now!*'

She thought he would refuse. He didn't move, but stood

regarding her intently, his hand still on the button that controlled the door, effectively imprisoning her.

'We'll meet again soon,' he murmured.

Giving her no time to reply, he released the door, got out and closed it again. In a rage she pressed the button for the third floor. Once in her room she slammed the door.

At that moment she could have committed murder. Salvatore had deliberately inflamed her desire because he'd been trying to subdue her as she was trying to subdue him. And when he'd made her half-crazy he'd shown her deliberately and unmistakeably that he, not she, was master of the situation.

The fact that she'd meant to do exactly the same to him made it much, much worse. Worst of all was the fact that her excitement, which she'd thought safely dead, had come searing back when he rejected her, and was now tormenting her again.

Tearing off her clothes, she got into the shower and ran the water as cold as possible.

'No!' she said. 'That isn't going to happen! *I won't let it!*'

Desperately she slammed her fists against the wall as the water laved her naked body. She wouldn't let it happen, but it was already happening. She would never forgive him for that.

But then she remembered how he'd trembled against her. The trap that had caught her had also caught him. The battle honours were even and the best was yet to come.

'Emilio Ganzi is a fine manager,' Antonio had said. 'He's run Larezzo for years and what he doesn't know isn't worth knowing.'

Helena could well believe it as he came to meet her from the motor boat. He was in his early sixties with white hair and a genial face.

'Everything is ready for you,' he said. 'We are so glad that Antonio's wife is going to stay with us, and we will all do our best to help you.'

The workers were gathered to get their first glimpse of the new owner. Some of them recognised her from her earlier visit.

'I couldn't resist taking a look that day,' she explained. 'It was so fascinating that I decided I didn't want to sell. I wanted to stay here and be part of Larezzo.'

They liked her for that. They liked her even more when they found she spoke Venetian. But what really made her popular was the red glass heart she wore, and the fact that Antonio had given it to her.

He was remembered as a man who'd enjoyed riotous living: plenty of eating, drinking and loving. In other words, a true Venetian. Several of the middle-aged women sighed, misty-eyed, at their memories.

Then one of the younger girls gave a little shriek, pointed at Helena and whispered, 'Helen of Troy'. That put the seal on their approval. How like Antonio to end his days married to a beautiful model!

Emilio gave her the grand tour, similar to the one she'd already taken but deeper, more intense. When they had finished her decision was confirmed. She loved this place, and these people, and she was going to defend them from Salvatore with her last breath—or, more practically, her last euro.

That became more evident when she studied the books. Antonio had warned her that there was a loan against the factory, taken out five years before, and rescheduled twice. The firm was keeping its head above water, but the repayments were taking a big chunk out of the profits.

'The fact is,' Emilio said when they were alone, 'that our wages bill is too big because Antonio had a kind heart. People reach retirement age and they don't want to leave, because we are like a family. So he always let them stay.'

'Then they stay,' Helena said firmly. 'We'll have to find another way to increase the profits.'

Emilio beamed and went off to tell the 'family' that everything was going to be all right.

Then the bombshell hit.

The letter from the bank was polite but firm. In view of the 'change of circumstances' the loan must be repaid at once.

'I'm afraid they can do it,' Emilio sighed. 'There's something in the small print about change of circumstances giving them the right to nullify the agreement.'

'We'll see,' Helena seethed.

As always she dressed carefully for the aspect she intended to present, in this case cool, efficient and, if possible, unsexy. That last bit was hard but she did her best with a matching dark coat and dress. The hotel's hairdresser almost wept when she told him to draw back her tresses into a style as stark and restrained as possible, but he reluctantly obeyed.

'Now I look like a Victorian governess,' she said with deep satisfaction. 'Excellent.'

A call to Valerio Donati, the bank manager, set up an appointment for that afternoon. She arrived ten minutes early and was shown in at once. Signor Donati was effusive with compliments about her 'businesslike punctuality', but she wasn't fooled. This man had made up his mind and would not budge.

'Do I understand, *signora,* that your late husband did not inform you of the financial situation?'

'I knew about the loan, but Antonio said that since all repayments had been made strictly on time…'

It was true. There was nothing in the loan to raise alarm, and she had no doubt that the bank had simply seized on an excuse.

'How long do I have?' she asked.

'I would need to know something within a couple of weeks; either that you had raised the money or made some arrangement to sell the factory.'

A suspicion was growing in her mind.

'Thank you,' she said, rising to go. 'I'll be in touch.'

She walked slowly back to the hotel, sunk in thought. She'd been very firmly backed into a corner. If she couldn't raise the money she could sell to Salvatore.

'Am I going crazy?' she asked herself. 'Why should I think he has anything to do with this? Can he tell a bank what to do? Surely not.'

But somehow it was just too neat.

'What will you do?' Emilio asked when she recounted the interview.

'I don't know. I could just give in and sell to Salvatore. You might all prefer that.'

'But you're one of us now,' he said reproachfully. 'We thought you were going to stay.'

One of us. The words resonated with her. They were a family, and they had invited her in. She couldn't let them down.

Besides which, the chance to annoy Salvatore wasn't one to be missed.

She made some calls to her bank manager in England and he sent her some files online, showing the precise state of her finances. She was mulling these over in the hotel lounge one morning when a voice overhead said,

'You don't mind if I sit down, do you?'

Looking up, Helena saw a very pretty woman in her forties, elegantly dressed and with an attractive twinkle in her eye. She introduced herself as the Contessa Pallone.

'But you must call me Clara. I've so much wanted to meet the woman all Venice is talking about.'

'Really? But I've only been here five minutes.'

'But everyone knows who you are.'

'Antonio's widow.'

'And the woman who's holding out against Salvatore. Believe me, there aren't many who can do that. He's a powerful man and he likes everyone to know it. We're all agog to see what's going to happen.'

Helena laughed. 'I'm glad I'm providing the entertainment.'

She ordered coffee and they settled down for a chat. Clara had a light-hearted personality but beneath the exterior Helena discerned a shrewd brain, and she felt drawn to her.

'I'll admit I had an ulterior motive in approaching you,' Clara admitted.

'Of course,' Helena chuckled. 'They're always the most interesting. What can I do for you?'

'I run a charity. It supports a children's hospital, and we're going to have a fund-raising evening in this hotel tomorrow night. It would be wonderful if you could be there, and perhaps donate a piece of Larezzo glass.'

'I'd love to. I'm just going over to the factory now. I'll find the loveliest piece I can.'

She took the boat over to Murano an hour later and, under Emilio's direction, chose a large horse, made of clear glass, its tail streaming out behind.

'It's the most expensive piece we make,' Emilio said. 'We don't want to be outdone by Perroni.'

'So Perroni makes a donation too?'

'Every year. Signor Valetti always offers the best piece he has. He gives a great deal of money to charity.'

Helena thought wryly that was what she would have expected of Salvatore. He gave money, he gave things, and so acquired a reputation for generosity with the least trouble to himself.

'He'll probably be there,' she mused. 'And Clara must have known that when she invited me. Well, there's more than one battlefield.'

'Excuse me?' Emilio asked, frowning.

'Nothing. Please have this packed up and I'll take it with me when I return to the hotel.'

Next day she handed the horse to Clara, asking that it should be listed as a gift from Antonio.

She'd said that she approached this as a battle, and that evening she surveyed her wardrobe like a general choosing the appropriate uniform. White, she decided; pure silk, modest and elegant. The neck was comparatively high, the sleeves were long, the hem swept the floor. In short, it was the opposite of what she guessed Salvatore would expect. Tiny diamond studs in her ears completed the effect.

The reception was held in the huge downstairs lounge of the Illyria. Clara sent her son up to collect Helena and escort her. He was an extremely handsome young man in his early twenties, and they made a splendid entrance. Clara introduced her to the assembled company, who applauded. Helena smiled and nodded to them, while secretly looking for Salvatore. After the way they had parted, how would they confront each other now?

Then she saw him, looking polished and assured in evening dress and black bow tie. Despite her scorn for his character Helena allowed herself a moment to admire his appearance. Wherever he went, whatever he was doing, Salvatore would always be the most impressive man in the room, with his tall body that combined athleticism and negligent grace, and his handsome face. But more than these was his air of assurance, his assumption that he was a lion among jackals.

And the winged lion was the symbol of Venice. They were everywhere. From her hotel window Helena could see one atop a tall pillar staring out over the water, proudly announcing that this was his city, under his protection, and under his command.

There was no mistaking that look, she realised, either in the stone animal, or here in this apparently civilised gathering. The meaning was the same both times.

Salvatore had seen her. He gave her a brief bow of recognition and took the first chance to come to her.

'I'm glad you're here. Clara showed me your gift, and I wanted to thank you for putting it in Antonio's name.'

'Of course I did. After all, he was my husband, even though you don't see it that way—'

'Please.' He held up his hand. 'Surely we can put that aside for tonight? Let me just tell you that you look beautiful without you reading anything hostile into it.'

He was charming, yet there was also something unreal about this conversation. At their last meeting he'd incited her then refused to make love to her with a cool assurance that was almost an insult. Now he was behaving as though that had never happened and, as before, he was making her veer between opposing moods with alarming speed. One moment it would have been a pleasure to slap his over-confident face. The next, she found herself responding to him.

He leaned close to murmur, 'You know we're being watched, don't you? The whole of Venice knows about us.'

'But just exactly what do they know?' she said. 'Or—more to the point—what do they think they know?'

Salvatore smiled faintly. 'A nice distinction. I guess you could make them believe anything you wanted. It's an art you might teach me.'

'Oh, I think you know a few tricks of your own,' she teased. 'And I'm always willing to learn new ones.'

'Now you're not being fair,' he protested. 'If I said you were up to every trick you'd insist that I'd insulted you.'

'Of course. And the annoying thing is that if I said it about you it would be a compliment, no matter how insulting I tried to make it.'

'And you'd try very hard.'

'Without a doubt.'

They laughed together. In the surrounding crowd heads turned. Knowing looks were exchanged.

'Clara tells me that you always donate one of the best pieces,' she said. 'I'm longing to see it.'

'Let me show you.'

She gasped when she saw his gift, a large eagle, seemingly coming in to land with wings swept back. It was made of black glass shot through with silver which glittered and winked depending on the angle of the viewer.

'That's beautiful,' she said sincerely.

'It's going to have first place among the new collection that will be unveiled soon. I look forward to your own collection with trepidation.'

The new Larezzo collection wasn't completely finished, but she would never tell him that.

Next to the glorious eagle her horse looked conventional. She must have showed it in her face because he said, 'There's always a contest to see whose gift raises the most money for charity. You'll be an easy winner.'

'That's nice of you, but I don't think so.'

'I'll take a bet on it. Franco!'

A plump, prosperous-looking man near-by turned at his call and beamed. When Salvatore had introduced them to each other he said, 'Franco likes nothing better than a wager. Here's the deal: I'll wager that Helena's piece of Larezzo glassware will attract a higher bid than my eagle.'

'Name the sum,' Franco said in delight.

'Ten thousand euro,' Salvatore said at once.

The other two gaped at him.

'I trust my instincts,' he added. 'The horse is a very fine piece, as is all Larezzo glass. What about it, Franco?'

'Done!' They shook hands.

The action attracted immediate attention and a small crowd gathered around them, all wanting to be in on the action. Franco whipped out a notebook and scribbled down the bets, obviously used to doing exactly this.

'What are you doing?' Helena muttered to Salvatore. 'You could end up paying out a huge fortune.' Her eyes glinted wickedly. 'And then how would you buy me out?'

'But you're not going to let me buy you out, so it's academic.'

'I suppose it is.'

'Besides which, if I lose a fortune I won't be able to buy you out, and you'll feel quite safe.'

Never in a million years, she thought, would she feel safe with this man. But she only smiled and shook her head.

'I promise you, I already feel quite safe,' she said. 'I'm only concerned for you.'

He gave a rich chuckle that was a pleasure to hear.

'How kind of you to worry about me, but please don't. I assure you I've protected every angle.'

'I believe you,' she assured him sweetly. 'I doubt if I'd believe you about anything else, but if you tell me you're playing a cunning game, I recognise the truth.'

'And aren't you playing a game every bit as cunning?'

'I certainly hope so,' she said with mock indignation.

Franco had finished taking bets.

'Of course,' he said, 'it's understood that neither of you bids for your own item.'

'That's agreed,' Salvatore said.

'Agreed,' Helena added.

Somewhere in the background an orchestra struck up for the dance that was to take place before the auction.

'Dance with me,' Salvatore said, taking her into his arms.

CHAPTER FIVE

HELENA knew it was unwise to dance with him, but he'd given her no chance to refuse. His hand was on her waist, drawing her close to his body so that she could feel the movement of his legs against hers through the delicate silk of her dress. Then caution dissolved into enjoyment. They were both excellent dancers, spinning around the floor in perfect accord. Her spirits soared.

When the music ended he raised her hand and kissed it gallantly.

'It was a real pleasure,' he said. 'One I don't get very often.'

Another partner presented himself, seeking the honour of dancing with her. Salvatore bowed and retreated, leaving the couple to take the floor.

Her new partner was a fine, upstanding young man with a handsome face and easy movements, but now she'd danced with Salvatore it was like drinking tap water after champagne. When it was over she thanked him pleasantly and refused all further requests.

It was time for the auction. Clara claimed everyone's attention, commended them for attending and made a speech of thanks to the donors. She spoke of the fund-raising which was to provide money for the children's hospital, ensuring that it had the very best equipment. At the end of her speech—

'Finally, our two stars of the evening, Signor Salvatore Veretti, owner of Perroni, and Signora Helena Veretti, owner of Larezzo. As you all know, these are the two biggest and most successful glass works in the city. Normally, of course, they are deadly rivals—'

She was interrupted by cheers and applause, as everyone regarded the 'deadly rivals' with fascination, causing them to bow and smile, then exchange conspiratorial glances.

'Guess what they're thinking,' Salvatore murmured.

'Whatever it is, they're a long way from the truth,' she murmured back.

'But tonight,' Clara continued, 'for the sake of the charities we support, they have put their rivalry aside. That is— almost aside, for, as you see, they have competed to see who gave the most generous offering.'

She indicated the two glass figures, and there was more applause.

The auction began. One by one the pieces were sold for prices greatly above their true value and the fund rose to satisfying proportions. At last only the two glass figures were left, gleaming gloriously under the floodlights.

'And now, the moment we've all been waiting for,' Clara declared, stepping aside to indicate them. 'Which one shall we auction first?'

'Mine,' Salvatore said at once. He gave Helena a mischievous look. 'Let my rival see the price my eagle will realise, and tremble.'

She joined in the laughter, but she was feeling uneasy. Salvatore's magnificent eagle outshone her horse and everyone knew it. He would have no trouble defeating her.

One part of her said she'd fallen into a trap and he would make a fool of her, yet the other part refused to believe it. Some mysterious instinct told her that this man might be cruel, he was undoubtedly ruthless, but he would not be petty.

He saw her looking at him. 'Trust me,' he said, as though he'd read her thoughts perfectly.

The bidding began and mounted fast: quite rightly, Helena thought, but her heart sank as she saw the inevitable moment approaching. She gulped when she heard the final price, forty thousand euro.

Then it was time for the glass horse, and she soon realised that her fears were unfounded. The value of the pieces was almost irrelevant. The crowd was having fun backing them against each other, and as the bids rose and rose they began cheering her on.

But then things slowed down and came to a halt at thirty-five thousand. A groan went up, but it was broken by a voice crying,

'Fifty thousand euro.'

The cheer grew louder. The bid had come from Salvatore.

'Fifty-five,' came a voice from the crowd.

'Sixty.' Salvatore topped it at once.

'Hey, wait,' Franco said urgently. 'We had a deal that you weren't going to do this.'

'No, the deal was that we wouldn't bid for our own pieces,' Salvatore reminded him. 'There's nothing to stop me bidding against myself.'

'But you can't do that.'

'Yes he can,' Helena said through laughter. 'He can do anything he wants.'

'I'm glad you realise that,' Salvatore said softly.

'Seventy,' called a voice.

'Eighty,' Salvatore said at once.

'Ninety.'

'A hundred!'

'Going, going, gone—for a hundred thousand euros.'

There was frantic applause, but Helena was troubled.

'This isn't funny any more,' she said.

'You won. You should be delighted.'

'What about all those people who took bets with you? They're looking very disgruntled and who can blame them? Why should they pay you when you won by very dubious means?'

'Thus confirming your opinion of me, which should please you.'

'Salvatore, you cheated. You can't take their money.'

'You just said I could do anything I want.'

'It was a joke then, it isn't now.'

'Helena, let me assure you that your pity is misplaced. Every single person who laid those bets is extremely rich. Paying up will be nothing to them.'

'But that's not the point. Please, Salvatore, let them off.'

He regarded her steadily with a look on his face that she couldn't read. Then he said, slowly and deliberately, 'I don't let people off. Hell will freeze over first.'

'Salvatore—'

'They challenged me, and if they didn't bother to check the terms first, that's their look-out. I fight to win, and if necessary I fight dirty. I thought you already knew that.'

She stepped back from him in dismay. Until then the evening had been pleasant. He'd charmed her, showing her a side of himself that contrasted with everything that had gone before. It had been confusing but even that had been enjoyable.

Now she saw how naïve she'd been to think there was another side to him. He'd given a chilly demonstration of deviousness that was also a warning to her, and there was a wry look on his face, his lips twisted in what might have been derision as he saw that she understood.

'You bastard,' she murmured. 'You sly, devious, cold-blooded—'

'Save it. I don't have the time to listen.'

To her horror he walked away towards the table and turned, holding up his hands for quiet.

'Some of you are feeling pretty aggrieved at the way I won our bet. You're wondering if I'm going to say it was all a joke, and you needn't pay up. But you should know me better than that. Start writing now.' He paused for one split second before saying with a grin, 'All cheques to be made out to *the charity fund.*'

There was a gasp, then a cheer as they realised how neatly he'd hoodwinked them. Clara threw her arms around him in an ecstasy of gratitude. There was much hurried scribbling, several cheques for ten thousand euros each were handed in, after which Salvatore took out his own chequebook and handed Clara a hundred thousand euros.

Then he looked directly at Helena with an expression that clearly said, *Fooled you!*

She forgave him at once. She would have forgiven him anything for the sense of joyful relief that flooded through her.

He came over and took her hands.

'Let us go where it's cooler,' he said.

He led her out onto the terrace and saw her to a seat.

'You should be ashamed of what you were thinking,' he reproved.

'You should be ashamed of making me think it.'

'You should also be ashamed of your poor arithmetic. I bid a hundred thousand to win those bets, but if I'd accepted the losers' money I'd only have won seventy thousand, so if I were the schemer you thought I'd still have been thirty thousand out of pocket. That's no way to make a fortune.'

'But—what you did was sort of cheating, wasn't it?'

'Of course I cheated. There's no "sort of" about it. Some of them were only there to be seen with a contessa, and get a reputation for being charitable, while giving as little as possible to the hospital. So I tricked them into giving more than they'd meant to. Did I do wrong?'

'Of course not. It was marvellous.'

Salvatore laughed. 'I must admit I did gain something for myself.'

'What was that?'

'The sight of your face, especially the moment when you realised that I might not be a total monster after all. I wouldn't have missed that for the world.'

They laughed together, then fell silent. At last he said, 'I wonder if you can imagine how glad I am to see you tonight. I've wanted so much to talk to you again.'

'Yes, I've been thinking another talk would be good,' Helena said, smiling.

'Tell me how you're managing. Is there anything I can do for you?'

'Excuse me, I'm confused. Is this the man who threatened to drive me into bankruptcy so that he could buy me out at his own price?'

He made a gesture as if the memory pained him.

'I wish you'd forget that. I said a lot of things I didn't mean. You were right, I'm not used to being challenged and I didn't react very well. The truth is I admire you for having the guts to take it on, and even more for having the guts to take *me* on.'

'You might well, considering that it was you who galled me into doing it.'

'True,' he said ruefully. 'Sometimes I just talk too much and it comes back and hits me in the face. I got well served, didn't I?'

'It's nice to hear you admit it.'

'How are you liking Venice?' he asked.

'I love it, what little I've seen. Everyone's so nice to me, and I find the factory really fascinating. I'm learning fast. I'm even developing my own ideas. Of course, I'm very amateurish. You'd have a good laugh.'

'No, I wouldn't laugh. We're fellow professionals. Look, we've had our differences but what's done is done. What matters is the future and if there's anything I can do to help you, please tell me. I still want to see Antonio's place succeed, even if it isn't mine.'

Once she would have come back with a swift riposte, saying he wished her well only so that the firm would be in good order when he finally managed to buy it.

But the impulse died before the sincerity in his eyes and the kindness in his voice. Now she could believe that he was truly offering her his friendship.

'Well, there is something you could explain to me,' she said slowly. 'What happens when the glass…?'

He nodded, then embarked on an explanation that was tailored to her understanding, yet detailed enough to be really useful. For the next hour they discussed glass-making techniques, and when they rose to go inside she felt she'd had a valuable lesson.

'Goodnight, Helena,' he said softly. 'And remember, whenever you need help, I'm here.'

'Thank you, Salvatore. I can't tell you how much that means to me.'

He kissed her hand and departed.

Helena made her way slowly to her room, sunk in thought about the conflicting impressions that had assailed her tonight. One, above all the others, cried out for action.

She'd wondered if Salvatore was behind the bank's demand, trying to force her to the wall. After tonight she had no doubt that the answer was yes.

When Helena's arrival was announced Salvatore looked up with pleasure.

'Helena, come in. I've been hoping you'd call.'

There had been no contact between them for two days.

Now she appeared at the Palazzo Veretti, in the room he used as an office, glowing and beautiful and he rose, stretching out his hands to her.

His smile didn't fool her, nor the way he ushered her to a chair, then sat on the desk, leaning over her solicitously. He was expecting her capitulation.

'And here I am, with some news for you,' she said.

She gave herself a moment to enjoy his expectant look, before saying, 'I've been a bit preoccupied recently. The bank called in the loan on the factory. They actually wanted repayment in two weeks. I ask you, what can anyone do in two weeks?'

'Not very much, I imagine,' he said sympathetically.

'It looked as though selling to you was my only option. Well, I've just been to the bank and I thought I should come to see you immediately.'

'Very understandable,' he observed. 'I'm grateful for your courtesy. Did the bank manager give you a hard time?'

'No, he was nice, but there were so many papers to sign, and I didn't understand half of them. Never mind, it's all done now, and I'm free, *free!*'

'Well, you will be when we've completed the sale. Don't worry, I'll give you a fair price. I don't like to think of you worrying about money.'

'Oh, Salvatore, how kind of you to be concerned for me! But there's no need. I've paid the loan off, every last penny.' A delight in danger made her add, 'Isn't that wonderful?'

He put his head on one side. 'Is this the joke of the day?'

'I never joke about money, any more than you do, I'm sure. Here, these will convince you.'

She took out the official papers, signed, witnessed and complete, proving that Larezzo was now officially free from debt.

Salvatore's first thought was that they were forgeries, but

then his head cleared and he saw the signature of Valerio Donati, the bank manager, a signature he knew well. Everything was perfectly in order. Payment had been made in full.

His face was a careful blank as he summoned up all his reserves of control. They had never failed him before, but nothing in the past had mattered quite as much as this.

She was smiling as though this were no more than an innocent moment between friends, but he knew better. She'd come here today to flaunt her triumph, letting him delude himself that he'd won. Now she was doubtless laughing inside. Anger flared up in him but he suppressed it. How she would enjoy any sign that he was disturbed.

'Very clever,' he said at last. 'I underestimated you.'

'Now, there's an admission!'

'A temporary admission. It won't last. You'll sell in the end.'

'Oh, will I? I've heard of stubbornness but this is absurd.'

'Is it? Let's face facts. Are you pretending that Antonio left you enough spare cash to cover this?'

'No, he didn't. If anything his funds were running rather low in his last months.'

'Then you must have raised a huge bank loan.'

'Really? Perhaps you shouldn't jump to conclusions.'

'I think this one is safe enough.'

'Salvatore, you have a problem.'

'*I* have a problem?'

'Yes, you simply can't believe anything that doesn't suit you. It weakens your position because it means that your enemy is always one step ahead, knowing something that you don't.'

'The enemy being you?'

'If you like.'

She laughed up into his face as she said it, and for a moment he was invaded by a delight so intense that it almost drove everything else from his mind. He fought it. This was no time for emotion.

'Very well,' he said slowly. 'Enemies it is. But how foolish of you to cross me. It's something I don't allow. You'll discover that.'

'Oh, don't be so serious. I've won this round, you'll probably win the next one, then I'll win the one after—'

'And I'll win the *last* one.'

'Maybe. Shake?'

Reluctantly he took the hand she held out and held it for a moment.

'So you're still determined to drive me out of Venice?' she said lightly.

The sudden tension in his grip told her all she wanted to know. He didn't want to drive her out.

'Perhaps,' he said slowly. 'Or maybe I'll let you stay—if it suits me.'

'It always has to be on your terms, doesn't it?'

He raised her hand, touching it with gentle, seductive lips that sent scurries of pleasure through her.

'Always,' he confirmed. 'But here—' he glanced around his office '—isn't our real battlefield. It's the other one that counts, and there—who knows who the victor will be?'

Helena laughed. 'Shame on you. You think you're going to win that one too?'

'Perhaps that depends on what you call victory,' he parried. 'We may both enjoy finding out.'

'That's true. I'll leave you now. You'll need some time to consider your next attack. But remember what I told you. Beware the enemy—no, not enemy, opponent—'

'That's better,' he agreed.

He was still holding her hand, smiling in a way that disturbed her. The warmth was stealing through her again, making her smile back—*Like an idiot,* she reproved herself.

'You're getting out of character,' she said.

'What?'

'You're supposed to be angry with me, don't you remember?'

'I am—very angry.'

'You're absolutely furious that I put one over on you.'

'In a terrible rage.'

'I can see. And you're planning your revenge.'

'Not planning it,' he said quietly. 'Taking it.'

On the words he drew her close and kissed her, wrapping both his arms right round her, imprisoning her own arms so that she had no choice but to stand still, defenceless against anything he wanted to do.

And what he wanted was to caress her lightly, teasingly, each whispered touch a reminder of their 'other battlefield' and the thrilling skirmishes still to come. She relished it as long as she could endure immobility, then broke free and took over the kiss.

'Call that revenge?' she demanded. '*This* is revenge.'

She returned his attack in full measure, pressing close to him while her lips made silent promises that challenged his self-control, just as he'd challenged hers. It was a battle of the Titans.

'I must go,' she whispered. 'I have a lot of things to do.'

She moved towards the door, then stopped and looked back.

'Remember my warning. Beware the opponent who knows something you don't.'

She was gone.

That evening Salvatore called on Valerio Donati. He was always a welcome guest in the bank manager's house, and was impatient to plan his next move. But things didn't go as he'd expected.

'That's the last time I listen to you,' Donati grumbled as

they sat down to dinner. 'Call the loan in, you said. She can't cope, you *said*. In fact it was easy for her to cope, given who she is.'

'Who is she,' Salvatore demanded, 'apart from Antonio's widow?'

'Are you saying you didn't realise you were dealing with "Helen of Troy"?' Donati demanded.

'Of course he didn't,' his wife said. 'Salvatore doesn't read the fashion pages, or he'd have known that her face was everywhere before she retired. They say she was among the highest-paid models in the world. She must be worth a fortune.'

Salvatore smiled and made a polite response, but inwardly he was in turmoil, remembering Helena's words. This was the secret that she had known and he hadn't. She'd taunted him with it, and she'd won.

He left his hosts early and walked home through the little darkened *calles,* and as he went it seemed to him that Helena was with him, chuckling at how easily she'd called his bluff.

On reaching home he shut himself in his office and got on to the internet. The name 'Helen of Troy' brought up a host of information about her success at an early age, right up to her retirement two years earlier, after which she seemed to have vanished. There was no mention of her marriage.

Then he turned to the pictures, hundreds of them, going back years to the first shots of her as a teenager, on through her magnificent twenties, to her very last photo shoot. It was like being confronted by a dozen different women.

The first Helena was little more than a child, giving the camera a naïve, confiding glance. Then she was laughing, inviting the spectator into a happy conspiracy, modelling a revealing dress, but with a touching innocence.

As he went on he had the strange feeling that the happy spontaneity vanished quickly. Something in that baby face had changed overnight. Even through her bright, professional smiles he could sense that she'd become older, sadder, knowing. And it hadn't happened over time, which would have been natural, but suddenly, shockingly.

A memory disturbed him: Helena studying the two pictures of his mother, the one young and happy, the other prematurely aged by misery. He'd snubbed her, refusing to discuss a subject that was unbearable to him.

He rose to his feet and paced the room restlessly, trying to drive the memories away. Every day he fought to banish them, and it was part of this woman's awkwardness that she brought them flooding back.

He went out into the corridor and stood listening to the quiet house. He should go back and continue his research into 'Helen of Troy', seeking the weakness through which he could overcome her, but instead he wandered along the corridor until he came to the room that had once been his mother's. There he stopped.

How many times had he stood here listening to her sobs from inside, longing to comfort that anguished woman, knowing that it wasn't in his power? Somewhere along the line his pain had turned to a rage that was still with him, years after her death. It was there now, making him crash his fist helplessly against the door.

At last he returned to his office and resumed his study of his foe, starting again with the young girl, innocent, then imbued with a poignant consciousness that shouldn't have been there for years. For a brief moment he could almost have pitied her, but the impulse died as he went on through the rest of the pictures.

Now he understood the first picture he had ever seen of her, on the beach with Antonio, her glorious shape barely covered in a tiny bikini. Instinctively he'd known that this was a 'professional' body, professionally honed, tended, protected, in order to be put on show and make a profit. Up to a point he'd been right.

But she wasn't the lady of dubious morals he'd assumed. She was a successful businesswoman with a shrewd brain that told one story, while her appearance told another.

What an actress she was, sultry and sexy one moment, reserved and virginal the next! He stared hard at her face on the screen, the lips full and pouting, the half-closed eyes delivering an unmistakeable message.

Come to me—hold me—touch me—let me show what I can do for you.

But the next picture delivered an equally clear message:

Stay back—I belong only to myself—

He brought the two pictures up together and leaned back in his chair, trying to order his thoughts. The contrast in her different aspects affected him more than he wanted it to. It meant that she was a mystery, which placed another high card in her hand, and that he found intolerable.

She'd challenged him on two levels, personal and professional, winning on both counts. The night of their meeting she'd faced him as an equal, teasing and provoking, knowing her power, flaunting it as though he were just another suppliant at her feet. That was a piece of impertinence, not to be borne.

Now she'd also taken him on as a business opponent, meeting his financial strike against her with alarming ease. On that level too she must be brought under his control.

Only then did it occur to him to wonder which of the two was the more essential, and when he realised that he didn't know, alarm bells began to ring.

At one time there would have been no doubt which one he wanted more. Only business mattered. Women came second. But this woman was unlike any other.

His time would come. When he took her to bed and held

her naked in his arms, when he heard her cry out helplessly with the pleasure that only he could give her, then she would be no different from other women.

From now on he would live for that day.

CHAPTER SIX

Now Helena spent all her time at Larezzo, learning everything, eagerly absorbing information, enjoying herself as never before.

Her employees loved her for her passionate interest, her determination to protect the factory at all costs, but also the fact that she had the good sense not to interfere.

'Not yet, anyway,' she promised them. 'My time will come. For the moment I'm just going to watch you, and concentrate on making some more money to invest. No more bank loans. They're not safe.'

The cheer that greeted this told her just how well-informed her employees were. There was another cheer when she added, 'I may have to do some more modelling for the sake of our future.'

One of her workers was heard to murmur that she should have sold out to Salvatore, but was quickly silenced by the indignation of the others.

'Perhaps you should fire Jacopo,' Emilio sighed. 'You know what he'll be doing now, don't you?'

'Reporting back to Salvatore,' Helena deduced accurately. 'Let's give him something to report.'

After that things happened faster than she could have imagined. Leo, the young designer and her ardent fan, gladly accepted her instructions to create a piece resembling Salvatore's head, but done to resemble the devil, with pointed eyebrows and horns.

'How long will it take to produce it in glass?' she asked him.

'A couple of days if I work fast.'

'Wonderful. I thought it took you ages to produce your creations.'

He winked. 'That's what I tell Emilio to boost my pay.'

'You forgot you're talking to the boss,' she teased him.

He made a comical gesture of despair, and they laughed together.

'Do this for me and I'll pay you a bonus,' she promised.

Emilio shared the joke when she told him.

'That boy's a wizard,' he confirmed. 'He's created pieces in less than two days when we've had a sudden crisis.'

'What kind of crisis?' Helena wanted to know.

Suddenly the kindly manager was embarrassed.

'Ah—well, it was a long time ago—'

'You mean before Antonio met me, and was still sending glass tributes to other ladies,' Helena supplied.

'Something like that,' Emilio said vaguely.

She sighed in apparent disillusion. 'And there was I, imagining that he must have lived like a monk. Don't worry, Emilio. I have no illusions about Antonio. He was dear to me as he was.'

Emilio looked relieved and soon found something else to do.

The glass head was a masterpiece, unmistakeably Salvatore, despite the extras.

'Are you going to send it to him?' Emilio asked.

'Certainly not. I shall just leave it here, in plain view, where Jacopo can find it easily.'

They didn't have to wait long. A few hours later Jacopo was observed slipping into Salvatore's factory. Next day he returned to work in a scowling temper.

'Salvatore sent him away with a flea in his ear,' Helena guessed.

'That doesn't sound like him,' Emilio said doubtfully.

'I think it does.'

'Don't forget he fights to win.'

'Unless he knows he can't win,' Helena murmured mysteriously.

From Salvatore there was no word. He seemed to have gone to ground, meaning that he was more dangerous than ever.

One evening, as she reached the hotel the desk clerk told her that a parcel had been left for her. In her room she unwrapped it and sat gazing in awe at its beauty.

It too was a head, but not a recognisable one. There were no distinct features, just a general air of beauty and fair hair streaming back. Any woman would be proud to believe that a man saw her that way.

There was no note or any sign to show who'd sent it, but she called Salvatore, and he answered with a speed that showed he'd been waiting. As soon as she heard his voice she said, 'I give in.'

'What—*exactly*—does that mean?' he asked with exaggerated caution.

'It means you're better at this than I am. It means you wrong-footed me. It means thank you, it's beautiful.'

'I hoped you'd like it,' he said warmly. 'Are you free to have dinner with me tonight? I know a restaurant that I think you would enjoy.'

'That sounds lovely.'

This time there was no gondolier. Salvatore came to the hotel on foot. By chance Helena was looking out of her window and had a long view of him approaching. She watched as he crossed a small bridge, pausing at the top to lean on the rail and look out over the lagoon.

She drew back, enjoying the chance to study him without his knowing. Hostility apart, she had to admit that with this man nature had distributed her gifts unjustly. There were better men in the world, good, civilised men with kindly natures, who deserved the best. Yet women would overlook them in favour of an arrogant schemer, who couldn't be trusted an inch, for no better reason than that he seemed to embody all masculine attraction in himself.

From this distance she could see what hadn't been so clear before, that his legs were long like an athlete's, and he moved with a careless grace that almost, but not quite, concealed his power.

At the thought of that power a tremor of excitement ran through her, warning her that she'd started on a dangerous road. She wanted him. She was honest enough to admit that to herself. She wanted that body and whatever it could offer to her own body. She wanted his hands on her, touching her intimately in the places that he'd brought alive just by his presence, and bringing them even more alive by the skill of his caresses.

Her head was on guard against him, but her flesh refused to be cautious. Nature had designed him to give her pleasure, and she would make him fulfil nature's purpose or live desolate for the rest of her days.

While she watched he straightened up and turned to finish the journey to the hotel. A few moments later she went down to greet him with a bland smile that gave no hint of the turmoil within.

He escorted her a short walk to a tiny restaurant, where he led her out into the garden and towards a small table in the far corner, lit only by a candle and a few fairy lights overhead.

'Did I make a good choice?' Salvatore asked. 'Of course it's not a fine, luxurious place—'

'All the better for that. It's charming. Thank you for not trying to overwhelm me with finery.'

'That would be very foolish of me, wouldn't it? I can't compete with "Helen of Troy".'

'So you know about that?'

'Yes—finally. Everyone else in Venice seems to have known about it first. And I must admit, you tried to warn me that there was something I didn't know, but I just charged on, didn't I? And I got my just deserts.'

She studied him for any trace of irony, but failed to find it. While she was still trying to make her mind up a waiter appeared with a bottle of champagne.

'The very finest, *signor,* just as you said.'

'Don't be fooled by the modest appearance of this place,' Salvatore told her. 'Their cellar is the best.'

When the waiter had gone he raised his glass to her.

'I salute you,' he said. 'And I congratulate you.'

'Shouldn't I be congratulating you for the neat trick you pulled?'

'I never intended to pull one. Jacopo isn't in my pay. He used to work for me, but I fired him for laziness. He got a job with Larezzo, but I gather it doesn't pay so well, and he persuaded himself that he could get back into my good books by spying on you. I've never encouraged him, but when he saw that head he took a picture of it and hurried to see me, saying I was being slandered.'

'Slandered? How?'

'That head shows me as the devil.'

Helena's lips twitched. 'Yes, but where's the slander?'

He grinned. 'Thanks, you've just confirmed what I thought. You didn't leave it out by accident. Jacopo was supposed to find it. In fact, he did exactly what you meant him to—which is what men usually do, of course.'

She smiled and moved in closer so that he could feel her breath on his face, murmuring softly, 'You don't really expect me to answer that, do you?'

She saw by his face that she'd given him precisely the hard time she'd intended. His voice was shaking as he moved towards her and replied, 'No answer necessary.'

He laid his lips softly on her cheek, let them drift to her mouth for the lightest possible touch, and withdrew.

'You just proved it,' she whispered.

'Did I?'

'That was what I meant you to do.'

'Your wish is my command.'

Helena groaned. 'Here's the waiter.'

They sat in well-behaved silence while he refilled the champagne glasses, laid out the menu and made a few suggestions. By the time he left the moment had passed, and they sipped champagne with perfect propriety.

'To let you enjoy the full extent of your victory,' Salvatore resumed, 'I'll tell you that when I realised how financially successful you must have been for years I was appalled at my own temerity in daring to challenge you. How I could have been so deluded—?'

'Oh, shut up,' she said, doubled up with laughter. 'You don't fool me with that stuff.'

'Well, I thought it was worth a try,' he said, abandoning the act and adding his laughter to hers.

A *frisson* of excitement went through her, making her heart beat with apprehension. How could she have forgotten that laughter was the most dangerous thing on earth between a man and a woman? More perilous than desire because more likely to spring on you suddenly.

She was helplessly off-guard now, caught in the delight of feeling their minds in tune, even if only briefly. It was almost a relief when the waiter returned and they got down to the serious business of ordering.

Suddenly he said, 'If I'm honest I'll admit that I'm glad we're at a standstill, because that means you'll stay in Venice.

And I really want you to stay.' He met her eyes. 'You're not going to ask me why, are you?'

'No, I'm not going to do that.'

'We have unfinished business, and I don't mean the glass factory.'

She hadn't meant to give him the satisfaction of agreeing, but she found herself nodding. It was almost as though he'd hypnotised her into wanting whatever he wanted. But in truth she knew that the spell came from within herself as much as from him.

'Tell me,' he said after a moment, 'were you really going to release that devil head to the public?'

'Of course not. I knew you'd get to hear of it, but I hadn't expected your answer to be so neat. I'm going to treasure that lovely piece.'

'I hope you're going to give me mine.'

'Actually I thought I'd auction it,' she said mischievously. 'It should raise a fortune.'

'Try it. Just try it.'

'What would you do? Sue me for violating your personal copyright?'

His voice was soft and vibrant.

'There are many things about you that trouble me, Helena, but that's the least of them.'

'I'm glad to hear it.' She met his eyes and was stunned almost to silence by the unmistakeable message she found there.

'Am I still doing what you meant me to do?' he asked.

'Definitely, but since it's mutual we can say that battle honours are even.'

'So far,' he pointed out.

'Yes, so far. The preliminary skirmish has been interesting, but it's not the whole war.'

'Perhaps the part that's still to come won't be a war,' he suggested.

'Oh, I think it will. More fun that way!'

He nodded. 'My own feelings exactly. So why don't I start by making a raid on enemy territory? I think I'd better come back with you tonight, and secure possession of "my" head.'

'Yes, it is rather revealing, isn't it?'

He raised his glass.

'To a long—a very long—truce,' he said.

'Armed truce?' she asked, raising hers.

'Whichever you think most enjoyable.'

'Armed, then.'

They clinked again.

She wondered what he was really feeling, and if he even knew the answer himself. They were both playing a game, but she was ready, and what counted was whatever was interesting.

And the coming night was going to be very interesting.

As Salvatore had said, the restaurant's modest appearance was deceptive. It served the very best Venetian cuisine, and Helena was soon deep in delicious choices, risotto with asparagus, risotto with pumpkin, braised beef with Amarone wine.

'You'll at least admit that Venetian cooking is the best in the world,' Salvatore urged, watching her, eyes alight with humour.

'I'm not sure I could go that far,' she said in a tone of serious consideration. 'I'm afraid the closest I could come would be to say—that it's the best I've ever tasted,' she finished wickedly.

'That'll do for now.'

'But Venetian glass is different. That, of course, is definitely the best in the world.'

It was the perfect choice of subject. As she'd hoped, he began to tell her about the interest they shared. It was something Antonio had tried to do, but he lacked a feel for history and he hadn't made it live as Salvatore did easily.

'Venice stands poised between east and west,' he said, 'and in many ways it's a city of the east. In the thirteenth century, when Constantinople was sacked during the crusades, some of the fleeing glass workers came to Venice, bringing with them techniques that made the world wonder, and beauty that had never been seen before.

'They were soon among the most important citizens in the Venetian republic. They could wear swords and do almost anything without fear of prosecution.'

'Ah, I see!' she said knowingly.

'Just what do you think you see?'

'That kind of power might affect some people. They'd start to feel they'd always be free to please themselves.'

Salvatore nodded, conceding her point.

'And you think such arrogance might have continued to the present day?' he asked with an air of innocence that would have fooled anyone but her.

'Sure to, I'd say. Remind you of anyone you know?'

'Possibly my great-great-grandfather, Claudio Veretti. He married into a noble family, which was common, as they were in great demand, owing to their privileges. The family originally owned the *palazzo,* but since they were spend-thrifts it soon passed into my ancestor's hands.'

'And naturally he changed the name and put his stamp on it,' Helena supplied.

'Naturally. In those days people of affluence didn't marry for love. They married to create more wealth, and what's the point of doing that if you can't advertise the fact?'

'Is that meant to be a dig at me?' she asked suddenly.

'What?'

'People of affluence marrying to create more wealth, which is what you assumed I did—'

'*No!* Helena, for pity's sake, I thought we'd put that behind us. I was wrong, I know that now. You didn't marry Antonio for his money. You didn't need to. The Press said you amassed a fortune during your modelling career.' He saw her raised eyebrows and hastened to say, 'I looked you up recently on the internet. The information wasn't much, it didn't even mention that you had married Antonio—'

'Nobody knew. We wanted to be left alone.'

'Antonio didn't even tell his family.'

'I think he knew you wouldn't approve of me.'

Sensing the approach of danger, he veered off hastily.

'As I said, little information but plenty of pictures. I practically watched you grow up, from pretty to beautiful to astounding. I guess that's why Antonio fell in love with you.'

'Not according to him. He didn't know me as a model. I'd already given it up when we met. I couldn't stand the life any longer. I wanted something else so I fancied myself as a businesswoman.'

She gave a little choke of laughter.

'Talk about delusional! I nearly let myself get conned out of every penny by a trickster. Luckily Antonio was staying in the same hotel and knew the man by reputation. He stepped in and saved me. That's how we met.'

She elaborated on the story, deliberately emphasising the details that made Antonio look wise and herself look foolish.

'The rest of the world saw me as a powerful woman who could have everything she wanted. Antonio saw me as a daft female, in need of male protection. In an odd way that's what attracted me to him. Shockingly unliberated, but I found I liked it. He thought I needed looking after. Nobody else ever did. For two years we looked after each other.'

She fell silent a moment, gazing into the distance with a faint smile on her face. Salvatore caught his breath as he realised this was the look he'd seen before, when she went into another world, from which he was barred.

'What are you thinking?' he asked gently.

'About him, the way he was, the silly things he used to say, the way we laughed together.'

Helena looked up suddenly and he was relieved to see that she was back with him.

'Don't be sad,' he said impulsively.

'I'm not. I'll always have him.'

She waited while the waiter cleared the course away. Not until she was contemplating coffee and cheesecake trifle did she say, 'I wish you'd talk to me about him. What was he like when he was younger? And don't be embarrassed to tell me about his conquests. There can't be many that he didn't tell me about himself.'

'He told *you?*'

'We were very, *very* good friends.'

Suddenly a drop of water landed on her hand. Then another.

'It's raining,' Salvatore said. 'We'd better get inside.'

They scuttled in and found a seat to finish their wine. Salvatore spoke to someone on his cell-phone.

'The boat will be here in a minute,' he said.

'I hope it's a nice, sheltered motor boat,' she said, for now the rain was pelting down hard.

'No, it's a gondola.'

'A gondola—in this?' She waved her hand at the window.

He grinned. 'Wait and see.'

She understood as soon as the boat arrived. A small cabin had been fixed on the top, made of a ceiling and corner supports, clipped to the side of the boat, with curtains around the four sides.

'Of course,' she exclaimed. 'It has a *felze*. Antonio said that at one time all gondolas had them so that people could travel in privacy, but now they're not seen very often.'

'No, these days the passengers tend to be tourists, who want to look out at the view, and a *felze* would get in the way.'

The gondolier pulled back the curtains on one side and reached out to help her in, while Salvatore steadied her from behind until she dropped down among the cushions. Then he was there beside her, drawing the curtains against the rain.

'Are you all right?' he asked, reaching out in the near-darkness.

'Yes, I think so—*whoa!*'

The sound was jerked from her as the boat cast off, rocking vigorously so that she reached out and clasped him.

'The wind is making the water a little rough,' he said. 'Hold on to me.'

She did so, and felt his arm go beneath her neck, then tighten, to draw her closer to him. In the darkness his mouth touched hers and she thrilled at the sensation, moving her lips against his, inviting him eagerly.

She felt his hand at the front of her blouse, pulling the buttons open, finding the slip beneath, moving further, discovering that she wore nothing under the slip, leaving him free to caress her breast with fingers that were both gentle and skilled.

He knew exactly the right touch to give maximum pleasure, and he used it ruthlessly to tease her nipple to hardness, after which he laid his lips between her breasts. She knew he must be able to feel her heart pounding. There was no way of concealing what he was doing to her, and she didn't try.

Instead, she paid him back in kind, letting her fingers find the place at the back of his neck where she knew he was sensitive. She'd learned it last time and now she used it to the full, relishing the sensation of his response, which he could no more hide than she could hide her own. He drew back a little, gazing down on her, his breath coming harshly.

'Don't stop,' she whispered.

At once he dropped his head so that his mouth was against

her neck, leaving a trail of heat and excitement wherever it moved. Her neck was long, swan-like, and he paid it the tribute of total attention, taking his time, not moving on until he was sure of her pleasure.

'Helena…' His voice sounded as she had never heard it before.

'Yes,' she murmured.

But suddenly there was a slight bump as the gondola came to a halt.

'We've reached the hotel,' Salvatore said raggedly. 'We have to become respectable citizens again.'

She clutched him. 'I'm not sure I can manage that.'

'Neither am I, but we'll have to pretend.'

He began to fasten her buttons. His hands were shaking.

'I think I'm just about ready,' she breathed.

'Then come with me.'

Somehow they managed to walk sedately into the Illyria and across the lobby. In the elevator they stood side by side, not daring to touch each other until they were safely in her room. Then it was unsure which of them moved first, but they were in each other's arms, kissing fiercely, desperately.

He began pulling away her clothes, tossing them onto the floor. The buttons on his shirt opened easily, revealing the chest beneath, thickly haired, rough to the touch, exciting.

There were no lights on in the room but outside the room lightning was beginning to flash. Boats passed, their lights gleaming through the windows, then gone again. Here in the bedroom her body flared into new life with every touch.

She leaned back until she could feel her own long hair touch her waist, while his kiss went lower, between her breasts, and she clasped her hands about his head, unable to suppress a groan of pleasure.

The warmth that suffused her went to every extremity,

melting her will, making it one with his own until she had nothing left to hope for except that this should last for ever.

Which was exactly what he'd wanted.

The words were like a shriek in her head, warning that this was still and always a struggle for supremacy, and their fierce sexual attraction was simply another weapon for each to use against the other, at its most deadly when at its most glorious.

Her violent excitement began to die as a chill of doubt went through her. It was so long since a man had taken her to bed that now she faced the prospect like a virgin. She'd enjoyed the mounting passion, the teasing and enticement, but as she neared the moment of truth she knew she was afraid.

'What is it?' he asked, feeling her grow tense.

'Nothing, it's just—give me a moment. No—*no!*' The cry was drawn from her as she felt his lips against her skin again. *'Let me go.'*

He released her so suddenly that she staggered and had to clutch him to avoid falling. Desperately she realised that her legs were now too weak to support her without his help.

'You pick this moment to say let you go?' he demanded harshly.

'I can't help it,' she gasped. 'I'm sorry, I can't go on. This isn't—what should be happening.'

'I'd love to know what "should be happening" according to that cunning little brain of yours. *Look at me!*'

He gave her a little shake that forced her to meet his eyes with their look of grim condemnation.

'What should be happening, Helena? Should I just trail forlornly away like a whipped puppy because you've decided against me? If you thought that you were deluding yourself. I've warned you before not to take me on. You were very foolish to ignore that warning.'

'It's not as you think—' she cried.

'Be glad you don't know what I'm thinking right now. It would make you shiver. Who did you think you were dealing with?'

'It's just that I'm not quite ready—'

'Don't play the innocent with me. You knew what was going to happen when you walked through that door. You knew before that, in the gondola, back at the restaurant—unless I misunderstood what we were talking about.'

'Let go of my arms,' she said desperately. 'Salvatore, I mean it. Let me go *now*.'

CHAPTER SEVEN

To HER relief Salvatore released her. She backed away from him towards the tall window, but he followed her, speaking in a harsh, ragged voice.

'You didn't come up here with me expecting to hold hands.' Suddenly his eyes narrowed and he drew a sharp, angry breath. '*Dio mio,* I was right about you all the time. You planned this whole thing, you scheming, spiteful little tease. Is this how you get your perverted pleasure?'

She was about to try to explain, to defend herself, but she was stopped by a flash of lightning that came through the window, illuminating the room for a second, then vanished. In that dazzling moment she saw the man standing close to her, the magnificence of his naked body.

Her mind was sharp with bitter irony. This was the moment that had haunted her thoughts and her fevered sensations, when she would see the truth about him, finally discovering if her fantasies had been correct. And they were. He was everything she'd hoped, his legs as long and muscular, his stomach as flat, his buttocks as taut.

She saw the arousal he was fighting to control, fierce, threatening, promising. His chest was rising and falling as though the effort to stay in command of his desires was torturing him, but there would be no yielding, for this man never yielded either to himself or another.

Here was the fulfilment of the dreams she'd barely admitted to herself, and it had happened now, at the worst possible moment. For above all she saw the terrifying look on Salvatore's face; a look of sheer, murderous hatred.

It was like finding herself in an alien world. What she was seeing in him now was no mere annoyance at last-minute frustration; rather it was as though he'd been taken over by another man, one driven by deep, violent feelings beyond her experience.

Common sense warned her to end this quickly, calm him down, get rid of him as soon as possible, but she had the sensation of standing in the middle of a furnace. Far from being frightening, it was exhilarating, rousing her temper to match his, carrying her to unpredictable heights. Common sense couldn't compete.

'I planned nothing,' she snapped. 'But you're so eager to think the worst of me that you twist everything.'

'What do I need to twist? You've sent me one message throughout the evening and a different one now, and I guess I know why. This is how you operate, isn't it? Teasing a man, hoping to drive him into a frenzy?'

Temper drove her to say defiantly, 'What do you mean, *hoping?* I've never had any difficulty.'

She made the words deliberately incendiary. It was madness to provoke him, but she was too angry to think straight.

'Is that how you get your fun?' he sneered. 'How many men have you driven to the edge before you give yourself to them?'

There was a perverse pleasure in knowing that she'd confirmed his opinion of her. The madness that possessed her now drove her to needle him further.

'I never give *myself,*' she said deliberately, knowing he

would understand the hidden meaning. 'That part of me is my own exclusive property, and you won't come close to it.'

'You're wrong,' he murmured. 'You'll offer it to me, I promise you.'

'No, you mean you'll take it,' she accused him.

'I never do that. Any fool can take. The pleasure is when you offer—even against your own will. You'll end by giving me everything I want, and begging me to take more.'

'Try me.'

'Is that a challenge? Because I'm going to accept it.'

Moving fast, he slipped his arm around her waist and tightened it so that she was held prisoner, her skin against his, the feel of his arousal between her legs, reminding her that this could only end one way.

She pressed her hands against his chest, trying to push him away, but the attempt was feeble. Her will was divided, and he must have known that, for he didn't yield an inch.

'Too late,' he whispered. 'You shouldn't have dared me to try you if you didn't mean it. Challenge given and accepted.'

Only a few moments ago fear had undermined her desire, but anger had mysteriously brought it flooding back, and now it was stronger than herself. Her breathing came heavily, so that her breasts with their peaked nipples rose and fell against him, telling him everything she would have gladly denied.

'Why are you angry with me, Helena?' he murmured. 'We're playing your game, your way, your rules.'

'My rules,' she managed to say. 'Then I can change them whenever I like. You'll never keep up with me.'

'Try me.' He echoed her own words back to her.

He was moving as he spoke, drawing closer to the bed. She braced herself, expecting him to toss her onto her back and hold her down. Instead he lay full length and pulled her on top of him in a way that took her by surprise, giving the illusion of freedom, but only the freedom to writhe against him.

'What do the rules say now?' he asked.

She answered him, not in words but by fastening her mouth over his. Now all thoughts of the role she was playing fell away and she was driven by blind instinct. He was a man with a demonic power to seduce a woman, and that power was enticing her along unfamiliar paths to a new destination. It might not be wise to follow the lure but she was beyond rational thought, obeying the demands of her body.

For so long she had fought those demands, pretended they no longer existed, fooled herself that they were conquered for ever. Now that delusion was crumbling in flames. She wanted this man and no other, wanted what he could do to her and for her, and she wouldn't settle for less.

She moved a hand over him, reaching down until she could feel him, fierce and rock-hard between her fingers. There was might and power there, and the need to have him inside her was intolerable.

He touched her breast, pushing her slightly away so that he could see her face as though there was something he needed to know, then increasing the pressure until she was on her back.

As his knee came between hers, separating her legs, she had a last look at his face, and what she saw there surprised her. The hard look was gone, replaced by something that might almost have been confusion: no triumph, just a searching gaze as though he too was in an unknown land.

Then he was completely over her, urging her legs further apart until she could feel him seeking entry, finding her, driving into her with a ruthless power that sent her spinning into space. She groaned with the strangeness of it, but that was followed at once by the certainty that this was right. This had been inevitable since the dawn of time.

He was moving inside her, slowly, prolonging pleasure with infinite control, taking her deeply, then more deeply until there seemed no corner of her that he couldn't claim. She was burning up, going out of her mind with pleasure so intense that it was unbearable.

She clasped her legs behind him, then her arms, taking him prisoner and crying out to him to make this last for ever. She had a terrible feeling that it would soon be over and she couldn't bear that. She thrust herself back at him with all her strength, seeking more and then more, until the moment came and it was like annihilation.

She returned to the world to find that her heart was thundering wildly, and nothing was as it had been before. Nothing would ever be the same again.

She was lying on her back, one arm flung over her eyes, which she kept closed. She could sense Salvatore near her but for a while she needed to be alone with herself, free from his gaze that saw too much. What had happened inside her was as alarming as it had been glorious, and he was the last person in the world who could be allowed to suspect.

She took a few slow breaths to calm herself and slip into the character she wanted to present. Then she opened her eyes to find him sitting on the bed, watching her.

'Well?' he asked wryly. 'Are you going to deny that I won?'

'You won nothing,' she said quickly. 'In here—' she tapped her breast '—nothing. Because there's nothing there to win.'

He placed his hand over her breast where her heart was still pounding.

'A machine,' she told him defiantly. 'Nothing else. Ever.'

'That isn't true,' he said slowly. 'Why are you pretending?'

'I'm not pretending, Salvatore. A machine.' She managed a little scornful laugh. 'Don't scowl. Think how useful a machine will be to you. No inconvenient emotions, no tears when it's over, a woman who knows the rules and doesn't ask for more. No different from a man, really.'

'You're already planning for the end?' he queried lightly.

She shrugged. 'Everything ends, although not too soon, I hope.'

He inclined his head. 'You're too kind.'

She yawned and stretched, the very picture of a woman luxuriating in sensual delight. 'We have nothing to do but please ourselves.'

'I take it you have no complaints?'

Her lips twitched. 'None that I can think of. If I do, I'll let you know.'

He laughed outright at that.

'Perhaps I should be going now,' he said. 'I'd be reluctant to cause a scandal.'

He waited for her to ask him to stay, but she said nothing. Her eyes were blank and he realised, with a sense of shock, that she was simply waiting for him to leave.

He switched on a bedside light so that he could hunt for his discarded clothes, then dressed quickly, meaning to head out of the door, but at the last minute something held him back to ask in sudden concern, 'Are you all right?'

The life returned to her eyes. 'Never better,' she assured him brightly. 'But now I really must get some sleep. Close the door quietly.'

'I will.' But still he didn't move. 'Helena—'

She yawned. 'Oh, dear, excuse me, I'm so sleepy.'

'Goodnight,' he said, and departed.

When he'd gone she didn't move but lay staring at the ceiling trying to come to terms with what had happened. Her flesh was still thrumming with pleasure and satiation. Part of her ached to have him back, to pull him down into bed with her and let him bring her body the ecstasy that had come as a revelation.

The other part of her wanted to flee Venice, flee Salvatore, flee the joyous prospect that had opened up before her, because she was no longer sure she had the courage to confront its dangers. She was lonely, but to be lonely was to be free. To get closer to Salvatore was to risk loving him, and that would be the greatest disaster of all.

High above on the ceiling nymphs chased each other, laughing as they darted here and there, exchanging looks that were meant to tease and allure, until the moment would come when the chase ended in delight.

They make it look so simple, she sighed to herself. But it isn't simple at all.

She wondered where Salvatore was now, and what he was thinking. She tried to picture him walking home through the dark *calles,* rejoicing in his easy victory, saying he'd always known she was just like the others.

But the picture didn't fit. It faded before the memory of the concern in his voice as he'd asked if she was all right.

She reached out, to switch off the beside light, rolled over and buried her head under the clothes.

Down below, Salvatore stood by the landing stage, watching her window, trying to sort out his thoughts, but they were too much for him. Nothing in the world made any sense.

She had been like a woman experiencing passion for the first time. Helen of Troy, whose lustrous body was a byword for sexual allure and delightful sin, had made love with an air of astonishment and discovery that had stunned him. Prepared for skill and experience, he'd found instead something shockingly like innocence.

He'd always avoided innocence. It caused too many complications. Helena's attraction had been that she seemed like himself, cynical, wary, well able to take care of herself. Her own words, 'A woman who knows the rules and doesn't ask for more,' had seemed to bear that out.

But it was false. Her caresses had been eager but simple

and artless, with none of the calculation he'd expected. He'd
known women with those very skills, who'd taken him to the
extremes of physical pleasure, but then shrugged when the
time had come to part. Not one of them had inspired the
concern he'd felt for Helena.

'What mystery are you hiding?' he murmured. 'Who are
you lying to—me or yourself? And *why?*'

He stood watching for a while longer, listening to the soft
lapping of the little waves, until her light went out. Only then
did he walk slowly, thoughtfully, away.

Business in Milan kept Salvatore away for the next few days.
When it was complete he remembered further business in
Rome, and it was a week before he returned to Venice to find
a large parcel waiting for him.

'It came by special messenger the day you left,' his grandmother told him.

She was a thin, hard-faced woman, expensively dressed.
The daughter of impoverished nobility, she had married for
money and borne one child, Lisetta, the daughter who had
been Salvatore's mother. Guido, her son-in-law, had been the
object of her hatred, often with good reason. Now that both
he and Lisetta were dead she haunted the *palazzo,* urging
Salvatore to remember 'his position', and disappointed when
he didn't live up to her pompous expectations.

He opened the parcel in front of her and then wished he
hadn't. It was the devil head Helena had created.

Inside was a brief note:

*'I promised you this. Thank you for mine. It's beautiful.
Helena.'*

He concealed the note quickly, but his grandmother had
seen the head and exclaimed sharply, 'So it's true! There was
a rumour that she'd insulted you but I couldn't believe she
would dare.'

'She hasn't insulted me,' Salvatore said, examining the object with interest. 'It's a very fine piece. If I'm not much mistaken it was designed by Leo Balzini, a young designer I've been pursuing for months.' He gave a grunt of laughter. 'He's even managed to make it look like me.'

'Don't be absurd. Who could think that a devil looks like you?'

'Anyone who could see into me as far as she…' His voice faded and he took a deep, unnerved breath.

'What's that you're mumbling?'

'Nothing,' he said hastily. 'Just take my word that it's not an insult.'

'Hmm! I find that hard to believe. A woman like that—'

'Please don't call her that,' Salvatore said quickly.

'I've heard you say it yourself.'

'But she is technically part of the family and bears the Veretti name,' he reminded her in a voice that would have warned a more sensitive person.

'But we don't have to accept her, surely. Have you any idea of the spectacle she's been making of herself this last week?'

'She's a model. Naturally she draws admiring eyes.'

'She's been seen out in the company of a different man every night, including *Silvio Tirani*.'

Since Tirani was a buffoon who pursued one woman after another, vainly fancying that his wealth could compensate for his vulgarity, this did not elicit the reaction she'd wanted.

'I'll bet she sent him about his business,' Salvatore said with a grin.

'I know there was a scene in a restaurant, the last thing this family needs. We must ignore her, however hard that becomes.'

'I seem to recall that you were fond of Antonio,' Salvatore observed.

He heard her give a sharp intake of breath and recalled, too late, that these were unlucky words. Despite being fifteen years older than Antonio, the *signora* had become infatuated with his boyish charm, and been unable to hide it. Rumour said that was why he'd fled Venice, and it had become part of the family legend. But Salvatore had spoken innocently, and now he hastened to add, 'How would he feel about you ignoring his widow? I think it's time she met the whole family. It should have been done before.'

'You mean invite her here?' the *signora* almost shrieked. 'Never. I won't consider it.'

'There'll be no need for you to do so,' Salvatore said coldly. 'In my own house *I* extend the invitations.'

When he spoke like that she knew better than to argue. She walked away in a furious temper, turning at the door to hurl back the words, 'I think you must have taken leave of your senses.'

He waited until she'd stormed out before murmuring, 'I'm beginning to think I have.'

It was easy to be indifferent if you worked at it. Helena had discovered this in her past life, and surely, she reasoned, it was simply a matter of being strong-minded again.

The problem of what to do after her night with Salvatore had been solved by discovering that she still had the glass head she promised him. She packed it up and sent it over with a note that was friendly but not effusive, then waited for him to contact her.

As the days passed without a word from him she faced the bleak facts: Salvatore had taken what he wanted, proved his worst prejudices right to his own satisfaction, and snubbed her by way of making his point.

Day after day she went to the factory and concentrated all her might on learning the business, managing for hours on end not to think of him. It was only at night that there was no protection from memories of his body against hers, inside hers, and the humiliation of wondering what he'd been thinking all the time.

The brief moments afterwards, when he'd seemed concerned for her, had been an illusion. Since then he'd shown his true contempt by his silence.

At last she learned through the Venice grapevine that Salvatore had left the city early next morning. The trip seemed to take everyone by surprise.

'It came out of the blue,' Emilio said as they shared a snack at the factory. 'Apparently his secretary had to cancel several meetings.'

'Does anyone know when he's coming back?' Helena asked indifferently.

'It seems not. He could be gone for ages. Let's hope so, because then we'll be safe from any action he could take against us. Always look on the bright side.'

'Yes,' Helena said tonelessly. 'Let's look on the bright side.'

She would stay late at work, stretching the day as long as possible, but eventually she had to face the evening. Her fame had grown throughout the city, and there was always someone to dine with, if she wished. But then it would be time for her to go to bed, hoping to sleep, but often lying awake, trying to blot out the picture show in her head.

It didn't work. The tormenting images were always there, and the memory of even more tormenting sensations. She would shut her eyes and curl up into a ball, shivering.

But she never wept. Never.

The heavy, embossed invitation was glittering and formal.

Signora Helena Veretti was invited to be Signor Salvatore Veretti's guest on the vessel *Herana* for the Festa della Sensa, in two weeks' time.

'It's an honour,' Emilio told her. 'Did Antonio ever tell you about this festival?'

'A little. Let's see—' she pressed her fingers to her forehead '—it goes back several hundred years, to the days when the doge took a ceremonial barge out into the lagoon, and tossed a gold ring into the water to mark Venice's marriage to the sea.'

'That's right. These days it's recreated every year. A fleet of boats goes out, and an actor plays the role of the doge. All the great men of Venice take part, including the cardinal, otherwise known as the Patriarch of Venice. You'll be in fine company.'

'Assuming that I accept.'

'People commit murder to get these invitations. Think of all the networking you can do.'

'Yes, of course, I must think of that.'

While she was planning whether to call Salvatore or write a reply, the phone rang.

'Did you receive my invitation?' he asked.

At the sound of his voice all the good work of the last few days went out of the window. What had happened between them might have been last night.

'I was about to call you,' she said.

'I expect you need to know a little more before you give me your answer.'

'No, I'd decided to—'

'We'll have lunch. Meet me in an hour at—' He named a café two streets away.

A click and he was gone.

The café was small, cheap and cheerful, a world away from the elegant eating places she was used to. Salvatore was waiting for her at a table outside, overlooking a small canal, busy with boats delivering supplies. He poured her a glass of light white wine, which he'd already ordered.

Her first view of him gave her an eerie sensation of looking into a mirror. If his eyes told a true story he'd had as many sleepless nights as she.

He rose as she appeared and drew out a seat.

'I'd have been in touch before, but I was called away suddenly,' he said. 'Thank you for the head. I've locked it away safely to prevent my grandmother smashing it. She's indignant that anyone should see me as the devil. I told her that you'd explain it to her when the two of you meet.'

'You did what?' she demanded, shaken out of her composure. 'What am I supposed to say to her?'

He shrugged, grinning. 'That's for you to decide. I'll just act as referee.'

His smile lit up the world, although she tried not to admit it. For a week her thoughts about him had been bitter. Now she was happy just to be here with him.

'I was right when I made you a devil,' she said. 'You've got the cheek of one.'

'So I take it you accept my invitation? Good.'

'Hold on, I haven't said that.'

'Why should you refuse? Because it comes from me?'

He said it quizzically, making his face charming. She tried not to be charmed, but failed.

'Let's just say I'm deeply suspicious of you for asking me,' she said.

'But you're a celebrity now. Naturally I want to be seen with you as often as possible, for the sake of my reputation.'

'Will you stop talking nonsense?'

'I'm being serious. As a man of position I have to make sure that you're seen in my company rather than any other man's. I couldn't risk competition from—say—Silvio Tirani.'

'Yes, of course. I might swoon into his arms at any moment.'

'I live in fear of it. All Venice is talking about how you sent him out of the restaurant with a flea in his ear.' He added wryly, 'To be honest, I have a certain fellow feeling.'

'Oh, *really!*' she said with deep scepticism.

'You've given me a flea several times. Perhaps Tirani and I should set up a society, Helen of Troy's Venice Rejects.'

They burst out laughing together, and the warmth came flooding back, not just the fierce sexual heat but the gentler warmth of minds in harmony.

'Are you all right?' he asked, echoing the words he'd used before, wondering if she would remember them.

She remembered at once, and nodded. 'I'm fine.'

'I ask because—'

'I know. I was in a strange mood that night.'

'I didn't harm you in any way, did I? Because if I did I'll never forgive myself.'

His voice was gentle and concerned. So were his eyes, she noticed with a catch of the breath. Briefly the battle was in abeyance. This was Time Out, when they could be just people reaching out tentatively to each other, not combatants.

'You didn't harm me,' she insisted firmly.

'But something troubled you,' he said, still gentle. 'I wish you'd tell me.'

For a moment he thought she would confide in him and his heart lifted. But then she gave him a beaming, confident smile and he knew he was shut out again. The smile was her armour. He'd learned this much about her by now.

'The only thing that's worrying me is the fact that you won—for the moment,' she said slightly.

'I haven't noticed you going out of business,' he observed.

'I wasn't talking about business. You told me—how much I'd enjoy our time together. And I did.' She raised her wine glass. 'Congratulations on your victory.'

'Shut up!' he said harshly. 'Don't talk like that.'

Once he would have triumphed in her words. Now they tortured him.

She shrugged and set down the glass, looking at him from behind her armour.

For the moment he gave up, knowing that in this mood she was beyond his strength.

'So you'll be my guest on my boat for the *festa*,' he said, 'and then at my home for the banquet afterwards.'

'Well, actually—'

'And if you've accepted anyone else's invitation you can just tell them you've changed your mind.'

'That's better,' she said with relish. 'Now you sound like you again.'

He was troubled, a feeling he was reluctantly finding familiar. It had been that way with him ever since he'd risen from her bed after a union that had disconcerted him in ways he didn't understand.

Salvatore was used to being the one who made love only with the body, while keeping his heart to himself. His experience of desire was that no matter how mysterious a woman seemed before they went to bed her mystery vanished when he'd brought her to climax. Then she said and did the same as every other woman, grasping hold of him when he wanted to leave, trying to prolong the relationship when it was dead, speaking of love to a man who didn't want to hear, refusing to recognise reality.

But Helena had turned away, content to let him go, seemingly indifferent. He'd found himself with thoughts that had never troubled him in the past, and had left the city to escape them. During his absence she'd sent the glass head with a polite note, but apparently made no other attempt to contact him at work or at home. He was puzzled.

She'd said she had no heart to give, and he was beginning to wonder if it was the truth. It had never mattered before.

'My family have a great desire to meet you,' he said. 'After all, you're one of us now. Yes, I understand why you give me that disbelieving look, but there are a lot of Verettis and they're not all as bad as me. At least give them the chance to welcome you.'

'Of course,' she said politely. 'I shall be very pleased to meet Antonio's family.'

A silence fell between them. She leaned back, eyes closed, enjoying the sun on her face, and he watched her, wondering what she was thinking.

'Helena…'

She looked up, meeting his gaze, meeting his thoughts, discovering them to be the same as her own. So intense was the experience that she could almost feel his hands on her body, touching it as it had never been touched before, as she'd never allowed it to be touched before.

Suddenly she was angry. How dared he make time and space disappear and take her into a new dimension just by looking at her? Who the hell did he think he was?

'Helena—'

'Yes?' she asked glacially.

'I'd like…' He seemed to be having difficulty getting the words out. 'I'd like to show you my boat, and explain something of what will happen at the *festa*. Perhaps tomorrow.'

'I'm afraid it will have to be another day,' she said. 'I have people coming to the factory and—you know how it is…'

She fell silent.

'Another time, then,' he agreed.

'In fact I should be getting back. I have a mass of work to do. I look forward to the *festa*.'

She rose, gave him a brilliant smile, and walked away.

He watched her go, wondering at the ease with which she could tangle his thoughts and sap his will. She'd just informed him that the next move would be hers, and she would make him wait for it.

Another new experience.

CHAPTER EIGHT

For two days it was a stand-off, both knowing what the next move of the game must be, both wondering who would crack first.

Going through the hotel lobby one morning, Helena was hailed by the young man at the information desk.

'You joined the tourist trip to Larezzo, *signora*. I thought you might be interested in the trip to Perroni. It will depart in ten minutes.'

She'd been about to head for Murano anyway. Now an imp of mischief prompted her to say, 'This is Wednesday, isn't it? Hm!'

'Does that make a difference, *signora?*'

It did. She knew that Salvatore was always at the factory on Wednesdays.

'No, not at all,' she said. 'Yes, I'd like to join the trip.'

She called Emilio, explaining that she wouldn't be there today, and went out to join the others on the boat. She was smiling as they sped across the lagoon.

She had to admit that Salvatore's factory was impressive. Larger than Larezzo, it had all the most modern equipment, so their guide assured them.

Out of the corner of her eye she noticed a couple of the

workmen nudge each other, staring in her direction. Salvatore would know of her presence within a few minutes.

'This is the new oven, delivered only two months ago,' the guide declared. 'It's state-of-the-art, and none of our competitors has one.'

'But I dare say Larezzo will have one by tomorrow,' said a voice behind Helena.

She turned and saw Salvatore, looking amused.

'Doing a little industrial spying?' he asked, taking her arm. 'You should have told me. I'd have arranged to give you a personal guided tour.'

'It seemed better to do it in secret,' she said demurely. 'I thought if I came on Wednesday you'd never know.'

His cynical glance told her that he wasn't fooled.

'As a secret agent you have a lot to learn,' he observed. 'Come with me.'

For the next two hours he gave her the grand tour, taking her to every part of the factory, explaining everything in detail. He didn't seem worried that she might steal his professional secrets, and when she saw the advanced state of his machinery she could understand why.

Emilio had explained that Larezzo had lacked investment during the last few years. Without actually saying that Antonio had wasted the profits self-indulgently he'd told her enough to make it clear. The factory had survived so far because its product was the best, but it needed more money lavished on it. As things stood, Salvatore had nothing to fear from Larezzo, and she had no doubt that he knew that.

But that was going to change, she resolved.

'Thank you,' she said at last. 'I've learned a lot. Now I must go away and think.'

'Found any useful ideas to steal?' he asked lightly.

She laughed. 'Any ideas worth stealing are well locked

away from my prying eyes,' she observed. 'Do you think I didn't know that?'

'No, I never underestimate you.'

'I've seen one or two things I could improve on.'

'Only one or two?' he asked in a tone of shock. 'Surely you can do better than that? Have dinner with me tonight, and we can talk some more. And give me your cell-phone number. You're turning into such a dangerous character that I may need to keep tabs on you.'

'Likewise.'

They exchanged numbers and he named the restaurant, the same one where they had eaten last time.

'I'll meet you there,' Helena said thoughtfully. 'There are too many gossips in the hotel.'

'Agreed.'

'I must be going.'

'I'm afraid your party has left without you. I'll call for a boat.'

'No. Since I'm here in Murano I'll drop in on my own factory—just to make sure it hasn't crumbled yet,' she finished satirically.

She walked the short distance to Larezzo, sunk in thought. Her employees saw her coming and scuttled out of the way, since it was obvious that she noticed nothing but what was in her head. When she came back to the real world she was in her office and Emilio was looking at her anxiously.

'I've come to a decision,' she said. 'First I must make an urgent phone call, and then—' she chuckled '—then I'll tell you *all* about it.'

Salvatore went to the restaurant prepared for fireworks, and intrigued to know what form they would take. Life without Helena was intolerably dull, and he was ready for anything. When she was late he began to suspect. Even so, she managed to surprise him.

The text message that reached his cell phone was simple.
'Regret can't make it. Work calls. Will be in office. Helen of Troy.'

Salvatore regarded the words with a wry smile, feeling both intrigued and entertained. She might simply have signed it 'Helena.' That she'd chosen Helen of Troy conveyed a message, one that was reinforced by her statement that she would be in her office. There was no need for her to tell him that, unless…

He made a quick call home to make sure that his motor boat was ready, and almost ran back to the *palazzo.* Ten minutes later he was speeding across the lagoon to Murano.

There was a light on upstairs and he found a door open at the back. Slipping inside, he followed the light above, until he heard something that made him pause.

A man was talking.

He'd expected to find her alone. Now he wondered if she really was working after all, perhaps entertaining business clients. Entertaining how?

Moving very quietly, he crossed the floor to the open staircase that led up to the next level. At the turn in the stairs he paused, hearing the man's voice come closer. Standing in the shadows, he could observe unseen.

Then the owner of the voice appeared and Salvatore grew very still.

He was a young man, no more than thirty, with curly hair and a strikingly handsome face. From here Salvatore could just make out that he was smiling mischievously.

'Come on, darling,' he was saying. 'Don't give me a hard time.'

Then Helena's voice, filled with laughter.

'I'm not being difficult Jack, honestly. I'm just not used to doing it this way.'

'Well, let me show you.'

He vanished, but Salvatore still heard his voice from a distance.

'Come on, do it like I showed you before. Put your arms over your head and lean back—that's better. You're still a bit overdressed. Can't you take something off?'

'No, this is as far as I'm prepared to go. Hurry up and take me.'

'But if you—'

'Just take me—like that, yes—and again…'

Salvatore's hand tightened on the rail until the knuckles were white. What he might have done next he never knew, for something intervened—a sound that shook him, made him stare.

It was the clicking and whirring of a camera, then Jack's voice saying, 'OK, OK, great, do that again—look at me—'

'Take me like this,' came Helena's voice.

'Yes, yes—like that—*lovely!*'

'Well, that should be everything. I wonder if— *Salvatore!*'

She came towards him, arms outstretched, a smile of welcome on her face. He returned it, taking her in his arms.

'I knew you'd be working, but I didn't know it would be this hard,' he said.

'It's all right everyone, you can pack up and go,' Helena called.

There was a general laugh, and for the first time Salvatore realised that there were several other people in the room, all female. Two of them were holding arc lights to illuminate Helena, and the third was the photographer's assistant.

Helena herself was dressed for photography, in a long white dress of thin silk, slit high at the sides, while the top plunged to the waist. From where he was standing it seemed to Salvatore that she wore nothing underneath, but, try as he might, he couldn't be quite certain.

The crew were packing up fast, but the photographer she'd

addressed as Jack said, 'I'd like to have another look around, to see if there are any more good settings—'

'Another time,' Salvatore told him.

'But this would be the perfect—'

'Out!' Salvatore commanded, handing him a wad of notes. *'Now.'*

They vanished.

'So you prefer their company to mine,' he observed.

'No, but I'm going to earn money with those shots.'

'In this place?' He looked around at the room, a bare wooden structure without decoration.

'They're not going to be looking at the place, just me, draping myself over it.' She went to a large beam, aslant from floor to ceiling, leaned on it and let her arms glide up slowly over her head.

'Like this,' she purred. 'And like this.' She raised one knee so that the silk fell away on either side, giving him a grandstand view of the most perfect, elegant leg he'd ever seen.

'And how much will they pay to see you like that?' he asked, moving closer and reaching up to trap her wrists.

'It depends how well the pictures sell. A lot, I hope.'

He drew her wrists towards him and over his shoulders, then took her by the waist, pulling her closer.

'Do you really not mind men looking at you, for money?' he asked.

'They're only pictures. Who cares if they look at me—as long as I'm not there to know about it? It doesn't matter what they're thinking.'

'But I'm here,' he murmured, dropping his lips to her neck. 'Does it matter what I'm thinking?'

'As long as you're thinking the right thing,' she whispered.

'I want to take you to bed and make love to you until we're both crazy. I want you to make love to me so that I know I'm the man you need. Is that the right thing?'

'Oh, yes,' she growled. 'That's very much the right thing.'

Her knee was still raised, so that it was easy for her to hook her ankle behind him in a gesture whose significance he couldn't miss.

'*Strega,*' he said fervently. Witch.

'Of course I am,' she murmured. 'I stir my cauldron night after night, thinking up spells to lure you in.'

His hands were finding their way through the slits at the side of her long skirt, seeking the top of her legs where she wore a lacy thong, so frail that it almost didn't exist. He grasped her hips, feeling around to the back, the swell of her behind, almost naked as the thong vanished in the centre. Moving carefully, he hooked his thumbs through the delicate material and, with a swift wrench, demolished it, dropping the shredded remains onto the floor.

Now there was nothing between her and his fingers, seeking and finding what he'd expected, the hot moisture that said she was ready for him. Helena gasped, almost overcome there and then by his skilled exploration.

'Now,' she urged breathlessly. 'I don't want to wait—*now!*'

She sensed vaguely that he was tearing at his own clothes until he too was half-naked, and then entering her with a swift, decisive vigour that sent pleasure screaming through her so violently that she grasped him to her, curling both her legs up and around him as if she would enclose him within her forever.

Forever. No end to the sheer physical joy that made the rest of life seem irrelevant. There was this and only this, and it must be made to last because she was yielding herself to it with a lack of caution that would normally have alarmed her.

But not now. She was strong enough for anything, even to look him in the eye when they had both climaxed, and say, 'Don't you dare stop.'

There was a couch in the office next door. He carried her in and they finished stripping each other before dropping down onto the narrow space that was barely big enough.

Her flesh seemed to have acquired a memory of its own, that had nothing to do with her head. Their first loving had left her with an intimate knowledge of him, so that her hands directed themselves to the places where a touch could drive him wild, and, once there, a kind of devil magic inspired them to caress and caress until he was beyond his own control.

He entered her with one fierce movement, seizing, claiming, conquering without subtlety. But then his hold on her changed, grew easier, less intense. Now he could draw back and look into her face as he moved inside her, still demanding but gentle.

'Look at me,' he murmured and saw her eyes open wide as though in amazement. He didn't understand.

'Tell me,' he whispered, 'tell me.'

But she couldn't speak. She could only look up at him, suddenly defenceless in a way that tore his heart.

'Tell me,' he pleaded again.

But their excitement was mounting again, driving him to move faster, harder until she cried out, clasping him to her as though she would hold him there forever. And he found himself wishing that she would do that.

As the world grew peaceful again he lay with his head against her, wondering at the web in which he was caught. She'd spoken of luring him in with spells, but her strongest spell was one she exercised unknowingly.

She could make him want to protect her. She could make him laugh. She was the most dangerous woman he'd ever known.

'*Strega*,' he murmured again.

She thumped him lightly on the shoulder. 'You're repeating yourself.'

'I know. But it's the right word. There's nothing else to say.'

She chuckled, and the feel of her body shaking against him filled him with delight. She followed it with a long, contented sigh that almost destroyed his control, enough to make him take her again at that very moment, no nonsense, no preliminaries, no manners.

Her fingertips were feather-light against his face.

'I wonder who won this time,' she said drowsily.

You did, he thought. You snapped your fingers and I came running like a desperate schoolboy, because I've spent the last week haunted by you, sleepless because of you, angry with you because you wouldn't go away even though you weren't there.

Something happened the other night that I don't understand. All I know is that I've been waiting for you to decide. Now it seems that you have, but I still don't know what's going on in your head, and that worries me more than I can risk letting you know. But suddenly you don't seem to have any worries in the world. Oh, yes, you've won.

Aloud he said, 'Let's call it even.'

A few days later they discussed the coming festival over dinner in a small trattoria overlooking the Grand Canal. It was tiny and basic, but its pizzas were among the best in Venice.

'The fleet of boats leaves from St Mark's,' Salvatore explained, 'so it will be a five-minute walk from the hotel. My secretary will collect you. Then we go out into the lagoon to the Lido Island, to the church of St Nicolo on the far side. After the ring has been flung into the sea we disembark and there's a church service.'

'Has this really been going on for a thousand years?'

'More than a thousand. The original idea was to demonstrate Venice's supremacy, and remind the world that the Venetian Republic would always be dominant.'

'And you haven't changed, have you? As far as you're concerned you still rule the world.'

'There's not a doubt of it.' He met her eyes. 'And if the world forgets, the world must be reminded.'

'You enjoy that bit, don't you?'

He took an unsteady breath. 'Can we not talk about that right now?'

'Do I strain your self-control?' she teased.

'Will you stop gloating?'

'Of course. I'll wait until we're alone, and gloat then. It'll be more fun.'

'As I was saying…' He ground his teeth. 'What was I saying?'

'Telling me about the festivities.'

'Yes, then there are firework displays, concerts, dinners. You'll come to the Palazzo Veretti for that part of the day. A room will be prepared for you, and I hope you'll stay the night. By the time the evening finishes it'll be too late for you to go back to the hotel.'

'Of course,' she said wisely. 'And it's such a long walk, isn't it?'

He grinned.

His decision that Helena should meet his family had been an impulse, soon regretted. His grandmother's blatantly expressed contempt had angered him, making him forget that he'd once judged Helena in the same way.

Now he would have given anything to get out of the occasion, guessing how many of his family would share the *signora*'s opinion of her as a vulgar, money-grubbing tart. Most of all he feared that one of them would insult her openly, driving him to her defence and revealing something in himself that he wasn't yet ready to face.

But since he was caught he was determined to show her honour in a way his family couldn't misunderstand.

'They're all eager to meet you,' he told her.

'I'll bet they are,' she said, wry but amused. 'Are the missiles ready for chucking? Will you supply them or will they provide their own?'

'I don't know why you should talk like that,' he growled.

'Liar,' she said mildly. 'You know exactly why I should talk like that.'

She regarded him with an impish smile, causing a confusion inside him that was becoming all too familiar: bang his head in frustration or succumb to delight?

'I misunderstood you once,' he said, choosing his words carefully, 'but that's in the past.'

'You mean you've told your family how things are between us?' she asked innocently. 'I mean—*exactly* how.'

He didn't answer in words, but gave her a look that made her choke with laughter.

'I'm sorry,' she said, touching his face. 'It's wicked of me to tease you, but I can't help it. You never see it coming until it's too late.'

'That's because nobody's ever done it before.'

'Nobody? Surely there must be someone in the family who sent you up rotten when you were a kid?'

He shook his head. 'Sending up rotten has never been a feature of my family life.'

'You poor soul. You've been really deprived.'

'I've never felt it as a deprivation,' he said firmly. But then he amended, 'Not then. Now I think some practice might help me to deal with you.'

'Don't worry. I'll give you plenty of practice. Now, go on telling me about what'll happen when I go into the lions' den.'

He tried to describe his relatives, many of whom would be coming in from distant parts of Italy for the occasion. After a while Helena's eyes glazed over.

'How many cousins do you have?' she demanded, aghast. 'I think you must populate all Italy.'

'We do. The numbers are frightening. But let's forget them for now. You'll meet them soon enough. They're fascinated by you. My young cousin Matilda is obsessed with fashion and says she's longing to meet "a real celebrity".'

Helena's lips twitched. 'But I thought you had lots of notable people in the family. A cardinal or two, a doge, a few aristocrats who married into the Verettis.'

'Yes, indeed. But to Matilda a *real* celebrity means you. And she's not the only one. Since we've been seen together my stock had soared.'

He said it half-humorously, half-wryly, as though his lighter and darker side hadn't yet decided what he really felt. Helena enclosed his hand between both hers and spoke lightly, yet also with a kind of pity.

'I'm sorry,' she said. 'I cause you a lot of trouble, don't I? Shall I go away?'

His fingers tensed suddenly, as though to imprison her, then loosened again, but still holding her.

Daringly she ventured, 'Shall I sell you the factory, and go right away for ever so that you never have to hear of me again?'

Slowly he raised his head, and his eyes were full of conflict.

'Do you mean that?' he asked quietly.

'No.'

'That's what I hoped.'

He didn't say any more, but neither did he release her hand. His attention seemed fixed on the Grand Canal, where boats were drifting along in the intense evening light. Sunset spread over the water, casting a fierce scarlet glow everywhere in its path.

'It's like the furnace,' Helena said. 'When you open the

Glory Hole you see that brilliant heat and for a moment it's truly glorious.'

But then the light began to fade. The sun's moment was past, and gradually the dazzling riches disappeared.

'And then it's over,' she mused. 'So quickly.'

'Yes,' he said, and she wondered if she heard him sigh.

The scene had changed to one of calm pleasure. Now the softly lit lamps were strung along the canal banks; *vaporetti* filled with laughing passengers chugged along the water, gondolas drifted on their way, each lit by a single lamp. It was charming, but it lacked the delirious joy of a few moments ago.

That could only ever be there fleetingly, she thought.

'Are you cold?' Salvatore asked softly.

'Yes, I'm not sure why, but suddenly—'

'Let's go.'

He walked back to the hotel with her, and as they reached the entrance they saw Clara, who hailed them with delight.

'Dear Helena, I was hoping to see you—'

'I'll say goodbye, then,' Salvatore said hastily. 'I'll be in touch again about the arrangements. Nice to see you, Contessa.'

He vanished, leaving Clara regarding his retreating figure with a wry smile that made Helena wonder what their previous relationship might have been.

Then Clara turned the smile on her and it became dazzling. Helena invited her up to her room but Clara insisted on staying downstairs in the hotel bar, thus suggesting that her aim was to be seen with the local celebrity. Helena shrugged and went along with this, amused and curious. She had the feeling that Clara had something particular she wanted to say.

The talk drifted to charity fund-raising.

'I still can't get over what Salvatore did at the auction,' Helena said. 'Tricking all those people into giving more than they meant to, then giving so much himself.'

'I'll say this for Salvatore,' Carla agreed, 'you can always count on him to give plenty of money, even if nothing else.'

A slight ironic edge on her voice made Helena regard her curiously.

'What do you mean by that?' she asked. 'If he gives generously, isn't that what really counts?'

'Oh, certainly. And he gives plenty, not just to my charity, but also to many others. But he's never visited the hospital, not even on an open day. Handing over cash is the easy way for him. He gets a reputation for generosity without having to give anything from inside himself.'

Since she had once entertained these very thoughts, Helena might have been expected to agree wholeheartedly. Instead she knew a surge of anger.

'But surely money's what you really need, and generosity is giving people what does them the most good,' she pointed out. 'If he funds a machine that saves a child's life, ask the mother if she'd swap that for a personal visit.'

'Well, you're certainly very hot in his defence,' Carla observed. 'I hope he appreciates it.'

'For heaven's sake, don't tell him,' Helena said quickly. 'He'd hate it.'

'Yes, he would,' Carla said, laughing. 'And you're very wise to keep it to yourself. We've all been a little in love with Salvatore, but one gets over it.'

'I have nothing to get over,' Helena said firmly. 'The mere thought of falling in love with him is amusing.'

'That's what they all say, but very few end up laughing. Don't worry. Your secret is safe with me.'

'There is no secret,' Helena said. 'And stop trying to make me say things that'll give you something to gossip about.'

Clara chuckled good-naturedly. 'Well, don't blame a girl for trying. I just can't believe I've met the one woman who's immune to his charms.'

'Well, believe it.'

'All right, I will.'

Clara drained her glass and stood up.

'Now I must be going. It's been lovely talking to you.'

She kissed Helena on the cheek and departed.

Upstairs in her room Helena threw herself on the bed and stared up at the brightly painted ceiling with its feverish depictions of passion.

What Clara had said was nonsense, of course. She was far too well-armed against Salvatore to succumb to emotion. The blazing passion he evoked in her so easily was another matter. It had nothing to do with love and she was content to keep them separate.

Then she recalled how annoyed she'd been at hearing him traduced, enough to make her speak without thinking. The feeling that had swept her had been—she could hardly believe it—protective.

Protective? About Salvatore, the man who was trying to ruin her, when he wasn't trying to subdue her to passion?

Was she mad?

Perhaps.

Once out of the hotel Clara walked a safe distance before taking out her cell-phone and dialling the friend who was waiting for her call. The friend, in turn, would dial other friends, and in ten minutes her news would be all over Venice.

'I've just been talking to her,' Clara said, 'and it's very obvious that she knows nothing about it—no, really, she still thinks he's a man of honour—poor innocent. No, I didn't spill the beans—we'll just wait until she finds out what he's done—oh, goodness, what a day that will be! Watch out for fireworks!'

CHAPTER NINE

Now the demand for Helen of Troy's services was building up. She made a flying visit to England for a photo shoot that offered too much money to be turned down. On her return she gave every worker a generous bonus, with an especially generous one for Emilio, whose loyalty had brought the factory through to its present strength.

The only flaw in her pleasure was that Salvatore had been called away on business, and couldn't celebrate with her. She'd planned that celebration all the way home, relishing every imagined detail. To be deprived of it had a souring effect on her mood.

She wondered if Salvatore too had become grumpy, and hoped that he had. But in their one phone call since his return it was hard to be sure of anything except that he was feeling tense.

'I look forward to seeing you at the *festa* tomorrow,' he told her. 'My secretary, Alicia, will call for you in the morning.'

Helena was waiting in the lobby next day.

'I've been looking out of my window watching the boats congregate,' she told Alicia. 'That big, elaborate one is glorious.'

It was a huge wooden craft, painted gold, the bow built high to accommodate honoured guests. Further back and lower were the rowers in medieval costume, and behind them the stern was also built high for visitors.

'It's called the Bucintoro,' Alicia told her, 'and it's where the mayor and the patriarch will travel.

'What are all the others?' Helena asked, for the waters next to St Mark's Piazza were alive with more colourful boats.

'Some are historical, some belong to Venetian sporting associations, plus a few military craft. Everybody wants to be seen at the *festa*.'

Salvatore was waiting for her by his boat, which was almost as fine as the Bucintoro, also gold-painted with rowers in historical dress. It was already loaded with people that she took to be his family, and who regarded Helena with interest, especially the younger ones. One of the young men whistled softly.

'Manners!' Salvatore reproved him.

'But I meant no disrespect,' the boy protested. 'Only a great compliment.'

Helena laughed. 'I'm not offended.'

Salvatore did not seem to be placated by her easy acceptance. If anything he scowled more.

'This lady is our guest and you will treat her with honour,' he declared. 'There'll be time for introductions later.'

He handed her aboard and led her to a seat near the front of the boat. He seemed tense, almost angry, and she was puzzled. She wondered if he was sorry he'd invited her, and was sure of it a moment later when a photographer appeared on the quay and started snapping.

A blast of music in the distance indicated the appearance of the procession heading for the Bucintoro. Leading it were the mayor of Venice, with the patriarch walking beside him, waving blessings at the cheering crowd. The music followed them all the way to the boat. They climbed aboard and stood acknowledging the cheers for a moment. Then it was time to depart.

The rowers bent to their oars. The boat trembled, and they

were away, followed by the other boats and the musicians, who had hastily scrambled aboard, and who played enthusiastically all the way across the lagoon.

Salvatore handed an elderly woman up into the bow.

'This is my grandmother,' he said. 'She has been looking forward to meeting you.'

The old lady was like a bird with her sharp face and brilliant eyes. She studied Helena critically and greeted her in Venetian. When Helena responded in the same language the *signora* looked displeased, as though she had been trying to wrong-foot her, and failed.

There followed a procession of nephews, cousins, sons. Helena lost track. All of them wanted to take her hand, gaze at her admiringly, then return to their womenfolk and explain themselves awkwardly. The women followed, looked her wryly up and down, then rejoined their men with the air of gaolers.

Exhilarated, she stood up in the bow so that she could see ahead to the lagoon, fast slipping away beneath them, and feel the wind in her hair. She wanted to throw up her arms to the heavens like a nymph offering herself to the sun, but she guessed that would be a little too melodramatic, so she contented herself with shaking her head, luxuriating in the feeling on her hair streaming behind her in the wind.

Looking up, she saw Salvatore's eyes fixed on her with an unguarded expression. She wondered if he was aware of it, but perhaps he was because he turned away at once, as though reluctant to reveal his thoughts.

But she knew them, she thought with a surge of pleasure. There were some things he couldn't conceal from her.

Now he was gazing at the horizon, as though unaware of the rest of the world. How well he fitted this ceremony, with its roots in Venetian dominance. Watching his profile, she had the strange sensation of seeing every proud Venetian grandee for a thousand years, asserting his superiority over the waves, over the world, knowing that he was beyond challenge.

Except by one person, she thought with secret delight. She had challenged him, astonished him, made him doubt himself. And he knew it. Standing there in the bow, confronting the wind and waves, he seemed the master of the universe. Only the two of them knew that the master had a mistress, that in her arms he became eager and longing, even if only for those few dazzling minutes.

Suddenly there was a cry of delight from a small motor boat near-by, and the frantic click of cameras.

'*Damn them!*' Salvatore snapped. 'What are they doing here?'

'What they're always doing here,' said an elderly man beside him. 'The local paper always follows the *festa,* so does the television station. And this time they have something special to focus on.'

He winked at Helena, who winked mischievously back.

'Salvatore, introduce me to my cousin,' the man demanded.

'You aren't precisely cousins—' Salvatore began.

'Oh, it's a useful term, covers a good deal,' the old man chuckled. 'I came today to see what all the fuss was about, and I'm glad I did. Signora, since Salvatore is determined to keep you to himself, I am Lionello. Your husband was very dear to me, and I welcome you to the family.'

'But how nice to meet you,' she exclaimed. 'Antonio told me about you and all the wicked things you did together.'

This delighted him. He introduced his wife and they all three sat down. Lionello flirted with her while his wife looked on with benign exasperation.

'How kind of the family to accept me,' Helena murmured to Salvatore.

'One part of it at any rate,' he said wryly. 'Every woman

here would cheerfully throttle you. Perhaps this wasn't such a good idea.'

'Nonsense; what harm can come to me with you to protect me?'

She leaned back against the golden rail, smiling—no, laughing at him. In his present mood it seemed deliberately provocative. He could not have said precisely what that mood was. She had spoken of protection and that was how he'd started the day, as her defender. But had any woman ever been less in need of defence?

He wondered exactly how things had been between her and Antonio. Suddenly it mattered more than he could have found words to describe.

The Lido Island could be seen on the horizon. Soon they were going around it to the far side, the place where the ceremony would be performed. When the boats were gathered the mayor took up the ring and cast it into the sea with the words, *'Ricevilo in pegno della sovranità che voi e i successori vostri avrete perpetuamente sul mare.'*

'Did you understand that?' Salvatore murmured to Helena.

'He said, "Receive this ring as a token of sovereignty over the sea that you and your successors will be everlasting."'

But the mayor had more to add. Spreading arms wide, he cried, *'Lo sposasse lo mare sì come l'omo sposa la dona per essere so signor.'*

'Hm!' Helena said wryly.

'I take it you understood that too,' Salvatore observed.

'Oh, yes.'

'Marry the sea as a man marries a woman and thus be her lord,' Lionello declared with a flourish, adding gallantly, 'But I'm sure that Antonio never lorded it over you.'

'He never even tried,' Helena declared, her eyes softening for a moment as she remembered the husband she'd loved in a way that most people would never understand.

'I expect you were the one in charge,' Lionello ventured with a wink.

'Of course,' she told him. 'Those were my terms. Complete submission on his part.'

'That's the modern woman for you,' Lionello stated. 'Personally I've always insisted on being the lord and master in my marriage.'

'Come away, you old fool,' said his wife, firmly removing him.

'Yes, dear. Coming, dear.'

When they had gone Helena looked up to find Salvatore regarding her sardonically.

'Complete submission?' he enquired.

'But you've always known that,' she said provocatively.

'Perhaps I have.'

She smiled, inviting him to share the joke, but his returning smile was stiff and formal. Wryly she reminded herself that he had no sense of humour, and then she knew a flicker of annoyance. This was a lovely day. Why couldn't he just enjoy it?

And yet she partly understood his edgy mood, it so closely reflected her own.

'Antonio would have appreciated the humour,' she said.

'While he was being submissive?' he asked ironically.

'Don't be silly. We took it in turns. He'd laugh and tease and I usually ended up doing what he wanted.'

'Usually?'

'Not always, but often enough. I loved his teasing. You know something, if more men realised how women love a good laugh—'

'More of them would play the clown to suit you?' he finished coolly.

She sighed and gave up. There was nothing to be done with him in this mood.

The crowds began to disembark, heading for the church. As the service began Helena looked around, remembering how Antonio had spoken of these occasions.

'Us kids used to get bored during the service and misbehave until we were thrown out. Then we'd spend the rest of the time playing on the beach. I was always a bad lad.'

'You haven't changed,' she'd told him, not once but many times. And he never had. Right to the end the perky devil in him, that she'd loved so much, had teased her.

Tears stung her eyes and she closed them, averting her head. When she opened them again Salvatore was looking at her, with a shocked expression.

As they left the church he came closer, murmuring, 'Are you all right?'

'Yes, I was just thinking of Antonio suddenly. You think I don't miss him just because I laugh and fool around—but you're wrong. If you only knew how wrong you are.'

'Perhaps I'm beginning to understand,' he said gently.

'He used to talk to me about this place, the lovely beach and how we'd walk along it together some day. Would you mind if I didn't come back in the boat with you? I'd like to stay here for a while.'

'I don't like leaving you alone,' he said, frowning.

'I'll be fine. I'll join you at the *palazzo* tonight.'

'All right.' She could tell he was unhappy about it, but he had to yield.

She bid everyone goodbye, promised to see them again that evening, and let Lionello kiss her hand. Then she stood watching as the boats drew away.

Although she'd never been there with Antonio she found that the beach was a wonderful place to remember him. Here she could be alone, walking along the golden sand that seemed to stretch for miles, listening to the tiny waves, carrying him in her heart.

I wish you were really here with me, she told him. How we'd enjoy the looks your male relatives are giving me. You'd just love that, and you'd egg me on to flirt with them, but then we'd sweep out together at the end, and you'd enjoy that more than anything. Oh, *caro,* I miss you so much.

It was strange, she thought, how the passion she'd found with Salvatore, after waiting so long, had done nothing to diminish her longing for Antonio. There was more than one kind of love.

Love. The thought halted her. She'd loved Antonio. With Salvatore she resisted the word, although it somehow crept up on her.

No, she didn't love him. He had merely shown her how to enjoy another side of life. It wasn't love, and there was no need to worry about it.

Having settled that, she made her solitary way across the island to the landing stage and caught the next ferry back to Venice.

At the Palazzo Veretti the banqueting hall was set out in splendour. Two long tables ran down the centre of the great room, set with the finest china and crystal.

Helena had dressed conservatively for tonight, in a gown that was long and black with a modest neckline. It was intended to be respectable, but it didn't hide any aspect of her beauty because nothing could do that.

She was seated between Salvatore and his grandmother, from whom she could sense a barely veiled hostility. The *signora* professed great affection for Antonio's memory and great pleasure in meeting his widow, but her eyes were cold as they flickered over Helena. She did her duty gamely, but she was glad when the dancing began and she could escape.

She gave the first dance to Lionello, then to his son, then

to one of his grandsons, a nineteen-year-old youth who sighed over her so blatantly that she wanted to laugh. He was followed by an endless stream of others, all competing for the right to hold Helen of Troy in their arms. Franco, the man who'd taken bets at the auction, glided past, saying, 'I'm going to make a fortune out of this.'

'Franco, don't you dare!' Helena told him.

'I can't help myself,' he pleaded outrageously.

'Well, make sure you give something to the hospital,' she called as he danced away.

She wasn't sure exactly how he managed it but he was soon surrounded by a little crowd.

Antonio seemed to be haunting her today. He'd been there on the Lido Island and now he was here again, reminding her of evenings like this when he'd glowed with the pride of ownership.

'And I did you proud, didn't I?' she whispered.

'What was that?' her partner asked sharply.

Startled, she looked up and found herself in Salvatore's arms.

'I excused your last partner who was making an exhibition of himself, and you,' he said crisply. 'You barely noticed.'

'I'm sorry—I was thinking about something else,' she said hastily.

'Something or someone?'

The cool authority in his voice annoyed her.

'Don't interrogate me,' she snapped. 'My thoughts are my own, although you don't seem to think so. You've been in an odd mood today.'

He knew it and was annoyed with himself for letting his feelings show, something he normally found it easy to avoid. All day he'd sensed people looking at her, and then at him, enviously, for everyone knew of their association. Once he would have taken those looks as his due, and enjoyed escorting the most beautiful woman. Now he hated to see other men gazing at her. He knew what they were thinking, how they were imagining making love to her, and as far as he was concerned they were trespassing on his private property.

'Why are you scowling at me?' she asked, trying to speak lightly.

'Because I'm not Antonio.'

'What does that mean?'

'Unlike him I don't relish the sight of you flaunting yourself before other men.'

'How dare you?'

'Don't act the injured innocent. You know what you've been doing.'

'If I have, I've been doing it for him, as a kind of farewell.'

'A very cunning excuse, but not good enough. He might have put up with it but I won't.'

'You won't what? You have no property rights over me, Salvatore. I do as I like, with your permission or without it. Don't try to order me about, because I won't stand for it.'

His grip tightened, drawing her closer. 'You won't—?'

'It's been a long day. I think I'll be going soon.'

His mouth hardened. 'Thus snubbing me in front of everyone.'

'Nonsense. It's late, I'm tired. I couldn't stop Franco taking bets, but I told him to give some to the hospital—'

'After, or before, your cut?'

Helena stopped sharply. 'How dare you? I'm leaving right now.'

'I would prefer it if you didn't.'

'Tough! I'm going, *now!*'

'Do you think I'll allow you to do that?'

It was an unwise thing to say and he knew it as soon as the words were out of his mouth. She knew it too, for she surveyed him, a wry smile playing on her lips.

'Why don't we put it to the test?' she asked. 'I'll head for the door, you try to turn me back and we'll see which one of us comes off worst.'

'*Strega!*' He'd called her a witch before, but then it had been a compliment. Now it was venomous.

'Goodnight, Signor Veretti. Thank you for a pleasant evening, but I must go now. I'll say my goodbyes to your family, and then I'll leave.'

'You will not!'

'*How are you going to insist?*'

For a moment she almost believed that he would make a fight of it there and then, but his control exerted itself just in time, warning him not to allow fascinated onlookers to sense any division between them. But his eyes were full of another warning, to her. This wasn't over, and she had better beware.

Formally he offered her the use of his boatman to convey her to the hotel.

'No, thank you,' she said gaily. 'I fancy the walk.'

'I'll escort you—'

'No, *I* will—'

'I offered first—'

The clamour of young men was loud, and Salvatore seized her arm, drawing her close to mutter in her ear.

'Are you mad to go with them? They're all hot for you.'

'Don't worry,' she chuckled, 'there's safety in numbers. If any one of them gets too near me the others will toss him into the canal. Goodnight.'

Waving over her shoulder, she sauntered off, pursued by an eager crowd.

As she'd predicted, her admirers behaved themselves, and once in the hotel she rewarded them by sharing a drink in the downstairs bar before retiring to her room, adamantly refusing *all* requests to accompany her.

An orchestra was playing in St Mark's Piazza, just out of

sight. It was a sweet, aching tune and she listened to it with a faint smile, wondering how long Salvatore would be.

Exactly an hour later the bell on her door rang as though someone was leaning against it. She opened to find Salvatore, his shirt wrenched open, his hair awry. He was through the crack in a moment, locking the door behind him.

'I take it you knew I'd be coming,' he grated.

'I had a feeling you might be dropping in.'

'What the hell did you think you were doing?'

'Being a good guest, entering into the spirit of things, having a good time.'

'You had a good time all right, and so did everyone else, with you putting it all on display.'

'If you mean that as an insult, Salvatore, you're way off the mark. It's my trade. It's how I earn my living, *putting it all on display.*'

That drove him mad, she was glad to see. She might be taking a risk, provoking him, but she didn't care. She was high on excitement, dizzy with power, desperate to provoke him further and then further. It had been too long.

'Of course,' she added, nudging him on, 'you have to know exactly how to do it—subtly is best.'

She was pulling at the fastening of her skirt, which was separate from the top. It came away easily and she tossed it aside—perhaps it had been designed that way. Salvatore was watching her, breathing hard. She backed further, reaching for her top.

But he beat her to it, reaching out to grasp the black silk and yank it away. A ripping sound, and it was gone. Then he was throwing off his own clothes, seizing her and tossing her down onto the bed.

'Suppose I asked you to leave?' she demanded.

'How are you going to insist?' he echoed her words from earlier.

His fingers were working at her black slip, tearing it off, revealing the naked breasts. Her delicate panties went the same way and at last he was there, between her legs, inside her, not seeking permission, just entering, completing her, owning her.

Something that had been raging inside her during the days apart came up to meet him, exploded then yielded, melting but ready again at once. Later she would regain her independence, challenge him, defy him. For now this was all that mattered.

'So now,' he growled in her ear, 'now what do you say?'

Slowly she turned her head on the pillow, meeting his eyes, her own full of mocking humour, murmuring, 'I say— what took you so long?'

CHAPTER TEN

'How did you get away so soon?' she murmured. 'I thought it would take you much longer.'

'One of my aunts took pity on me and told me to clear off because I was useless.'

They were lying in the dark. It was almost dawn and they had loved each other to exhaustion. Now they simply lay together, naked, resting.

'I'll have to go back soon,' he groaned, 'and spend today being a host. But the last of them will leave early tomorrow, and then I'll come straight here. I want to be alone with you.'

'That sounds lovely,' she said. 'But is it possible to be alone in Venice?'

'It is where I'm going to take you.'

'Where's that?'

He grinned. 'Wait and see. All I'll tell you is—wear sensible clothes.'

'Define sensible.'

'Shirt and trousers.'

Reluctantly he got out of bed and began picking up his clothes from the floor. When he'd finished dressing he sat on the bed and took her hand, gazing down at it.

'What I said about "your cut,"' he said awkwardly. 'You know I—'

'I know,' she said gently.

'I'd have said anything to hurt you. I'm afraid I'm like that.'

'So am I,' she admitted.

'I don't believe that. But sometimes a cruel devil comes over me and I give in to it.'

She sat up and rested her cheek against his shoulder.

'Sometimes the urge to make a dramatic effect is just too strong,' she offered.

'Thank you. That's very generous.'

She chuckled. 'Let me give you a tip about making an effect. When you get home, don't creep in. Make sure everyone knows that you were away for hours.'

He stared at her, his eyes gleaming.

'You mean—?'

'Then those eager young lads will know that you achieved what they couldn't,' she finished triumphantly.

'You're a wicked, wicked woman,' he said fervently, kissing her.

'I know. Isn't it fun? Now be off. I need lots of sleep before I can be wicked again.'

She spent most of that day dozing in perfect contentment. Next morning there was a message from Salvatore to be ready on the dot of ten. He was there promptly, driving a large white motor boat. His eyebrows rose when he saw her attire.

'You said trousers,' she defended herself.

'I also said sensible, not trousers that hug your waist and hips so tightly that—well—'

'They're the only ones I have.'

'Yes, I suppose they are. Get in, and I'll try to keep my mind on my driving. It won't be easy but I'll try.'

It was a glorious day, full of the sparkling delight of early summer. As the boat headed out over the lagoon she stood beside him, rejoicing in the feel of the wind in her hair.

'Where are we going?' she yelled above the noise of the engine.

'To one of the islands.'

She knew there were about a dozen small islands in the lagoon, places so small that nobody lived there, and as they went further out she guessed they were heading for one of these. Even so she had a surprise when Salvatore finally drew into a tiny cove. There was a small landing stage and a post with a metal ring to which he tethered the boat.

'It's so tiny,' she said, astonished. 'At least, what I can see of it is tiny.'

'That's right. It's about half a mile in one direction, and three quarters of a mile in another. When we've gone through those trees at the edge of the beach you'll be able to see the whole place.'

The ground sloped up so that as they emerged from the trees Helena found that she did indeed have a perfect view of the tiny island, including how the shore curved away on each side, until it enclosed the island in the distance. Looking around, she discovered that she could just make out Venice far away across the lagoon.

She stood for a moment, revelling in the perfect peace of this little place, where the only sound was birdsong, and the soft lapping of the waves.

'It's beautiful,' she murmured. 'Is it yours?'

'Yes. It used to belong to my mother. She brought me here when I was a child, and promised that one day it would be mine. She said it was a place of refuge when the world became too much. And she was right.'

'I can't imagine you ever finding the world too much,' Helena said. But she spoke without antagonism.

'Of course. That's the idea of a place like this. You can hide your weaknesses here, then emerge stronger, to confront people.'

It was as though he'd opened a tiny window into himself, giving her a glimpse of a different man. But he closed it again at once, saying, 'Let me show you the house. You can just see it there beyond that clump of trees.'

She hadn't even noticed it before, so modest was the building. No grandeur here, just a comfortable-looking bungalow with a couple of outhouses.

As they walked towards it he took her hand. It seemed a casual gesture, yet there was something pleasing about the warmth and firmness of his clasp.

'Careful,' he said, indicating a large stone in her path and steadying her as she crossed it. 'We're nearly there.'

Hand in hand they walked on to the house. Despite its isolation she found that it had everything necessary for comfort, including running water, light and warmth from its own generator.

'So you can run a main-line computer,' she said. 'I'll bet you do your best work here.'

'No computer,' he said. 'I have a cell-phone so that I can be reached in case of emergencies, and a small radio, but apart from that, nothing.'

With delight she saw that it was a place where a man could retreat from the world and be alone with himself. Or perhaps one other.

He showed her the kitchen, the freezer stocked with food. Then he unpacked a large bag he'd brought with him on the boat, revealing fresh bread, potatoes, steak and salad.

'Wait until you taste my cooking,' he said.

'A man who lives in a *palazzo* knows how to cook? I don't believe it.'

'Is that a challenge?'

'If you care to take it that way.'

He got to work while she looked around the bungalow, which was modestly appointed with two bedrooms, one living room and a place that seemed like a small library. The furniture was sparse, little more than necessities, and she wondered if he preferred this after the luxury in which he normally lived. It almost suggested that the man who felt at home here must be a monk.

But that wasn't so, she mused, remembering last night.

They ate on the terrace overlooking the sea. Far off she could just make out the shore of Venice, merely a thin line of buildings.

'It's good to get away before things start being noisy again,' Salvatore observed.

'Why are they going to get noisy?'

'I've got a new line of glass coming out and it'll be unveiled in a few days.'

'Oh, yes, mine's a bit later. Emilio's getting excited about it.'

'A lot of store buyers come down and half your sales will be made in that first week. You'll be all right. Your line is good.'

'I won't ask how you know,' she said wryly. 'I haven't forgotten how you walk in and out of Larezzo as though you own it.'

'Walked, past tense. I wouldn't dare do it now.'

'Hm!'

He laughed. 'You still don't trust me, do you?'

'Can we discuss this another time? I'm enjoying myself and I don't want to spoil it.'

'You're right. Business should be kept well away from this place.'

'I think it's lovely, a perfect little world apart.'

Salvatore nodded.

'I sit here some evenings and look over there where the lights are winking,' he said. 'It looks so close, it's hard to believe it's really so far away. And I can hear the bell in the campanile booming all the way over here. It's like being alone and yet being in Venice at the same time.'

'Living your life from within, and standing back to see yourself as other people do, all in one moment,' she murmured.

He looked at her quickly. 'Yes, that's exactly what I was trying to say, but you put it better. And I suppose you know more than anyone about seeing yourself through other people's eyes.'

His tone was friendly, without the defensive edge that usually tinged it, even in their lighter moments, and she nodded, happy to relax with him.

'You're right. Sometimes I feel as though there are fifty versions of me, and none of them are really me. Yet I suppose something of those terrible women must be inside me, or how did they grow?'

'Why do you call them terrible when they're known for their beauty?' he asked. 'Is beauty terrible?'

'It can be, when people look at you and see nothing else. It can be a curse.' Then she made a sound of impatience with herself. 'Oh, listen to me! There are millions of women who'd give the earth to have what I have. My life's easy compared to what a lot of them have to put up with. It's just that some-times—sometimes I think of their nice ordinary lives with children and men who work at unexciting jobs and come home every day, and love them for their own selves, not because of their looks, and I think how lucky they are.'

He didn't speak, but took her hand, caressing it softly with his own. Dreamily she wondered if this gentle, peaceful man could be the same one who enjoyed tormenting her to climax.

But he too had many faces, as she was discovering, and the knowledge bred in her a longing to explore further and discover the others.

'You must sense it too,' she said. 'People who think they know you, but actually they haven't the first idea.'

'True, but I can't blame them. I show them what I want them to see, and if they believe it, well and good.'

'But where does that leave you?' she asked.

He shrugged. 'Safe, I suppose.'

'But what price are you paying?'

'Perhaps the same as you.'

'Is it worth it?' she asked curiously.

'Sometimes it is. There are times when I know I've done the right thing in standing guard over myself. At others…' He shrugged again.

'But why do you have to stand guard? Would the world come to an end if you eased up, trusted people a little?'

'I've seen other people's worlds come to an end like that,' he said slowly, 'because they trusted, and then found that their fate wasn't in their own hands. That's something I'll never let happen to me. My fate will be in my hands and nobody else's, as long as I live.'

He spread his hands out before him, as though seeing them for the first time. They were large and powerful, but something made Helena take one of them in hers and hold it gently. He became suddenly still and she had the feeling that she'd taken him by surprise.

She too was surprised. Her own fingers were delicate compared to his, yet his hand lay in hers, unresisting, as though, just for a moment, all the power was with her.

Memories of their times together came back to her as she turned his hand over. So fierce, yet so gentle, imprisoning her, caressing her, doing whatever he pleased but making sure it pleased her too.

On impulse she tightened her fingers on his.

'Come with me,' she said.

He rose to his feet and let her lead him inside, to the larger bedroom.

They undressed quickly and fell onto the bed together. In contrast with last time he now seemed almost hesitant.

She put her arms above her head and stretched out blissfully, with a sigh that might have been contentment or expectation. At once he reached out, laying one hand between her breasts, and resting it there as though awaiting her reaction. Her pulse quickened but she stayed still.

Very slowly his fingers moved, inching their way towards her right breast, pausing, venturing further, pausing again. Helena smiled, daring him. Further, further, until his fingertips reached one nipple, already reacting, and teased it until it grew harder still.

'Do you want me?' he asked softly.

'Do you think I do?'

'Little tease. Answer me.'

She laughed. 'Don't tell me a man as experienced as you needs to ask.'

He shifted his hand to the other breast.

'A woman can say one thing with her body and another with her lips,' he remarked. 'She does it deliberately to confuse a man.'

'Then, since my lips can't be trusted, you don't need to hear from them,' she pointed out.

It was hard to speak through her rapid breathing, but she was enjoying this too much to let it go.

'True, I have another use for them,' he said before his mouth came down on hers.

His kiss was long and had a soft urgency that thrilled her. She yearned against him, inviting him to go on, but he seemed reluctant to do that, touching her softly with his mouth, then retreating at once, refusing to deepen the kiss with his tongue.

She felt his lips against her neck, just below her ear, where he knew she was especially sensitive, and shivered with delight. The sensation moved slowly down her neck to the little hollow at the base of her throat. There he lingered, now using the tip of his tongue to torment her deliciously.

'Aaaa-aaah!' The soft cry broke from her. 'Don't stop.'

'I'm not going to stop,' he whispered against her skin.
'I'm going to kiss you all over. Then perhaps I'll stop—or
perhaps I won't.'

She could almost hear him smiling as he spoke, and her
own smile seemed to rise from deep within her.

Now he'd moved on to one breast, concentrating intently
as he kissed it, now here, now there, now with his lips, then
with his tongue. A fire was glowing within her, mounting
slowly until she feared that she would climax too soon, but he
never let that happen, always drawing back just before she was
overwhelmed, then renewing the soft assault. It was a kind of
torture, but one that left her dizzy with exquisite delight.

'Don't make me wait too long,' she gasped.

'Be patient,' he commanded.

'I can't be patient.'

'Then I must make you.'

He drew back to survey her with a slightly mocking smile
on his lips.

'You devil,' she whispered, reaching for him and trying to
pull him over her.

It was useless. He resisted her easily, while the amused
pleasure in his eyes made her wonder if he really was a devil.

Desperate with frustration, she reached down, seeking
him, finding him hard and ready. But he thwarted her, seizing
her hand, then finding her other hand and drawing them both
up above her head, holding them down on the pillow while
she writhed helplessly.

'Let me go,' she said, outraged.

'No, I feel safer like this. Who knows what damage you
might do me if I let you go?'

'I know what I'd like to do,' she growled.

'Don't be in such a hurry,' he murmured. 'The best is
yet to come.'

He freed her hands but before she could fight him he

flipped her over onto her stomach, and began work again on the back of her neck. Here too she was especially sensitive and tremors of pleasure went through her, driving her previous annoyance away to a far place where she would think about it later. Maybe.

'Grrr!' she murmured.

'Shall I stop?'

'You do and you're dead.'

He laughed, and his breath whispered along her spine, making her gasp. Now her whole back seemed defenceless so that every kiss was a soft attack for which she was completely unprepared. There was no protection against what he was doing to her, demonstrating his power to drive her wild with caresses that teased, hinted, promised, but never fulfilled.

Protest was useless. She was his as long as he could melt her in the heat of frustrated desire, and he knew exactly what he was doing, drifting slowly down her spine until he reached her waist. And there, like any good general who knew that the battle was going his way, he brought in reinforcements. Without removing his lips from her spine he increased the assault with his hands, moving them over the flare of her hips, her behind, tracing soft lines that criss-crossed each other.

She thought of those hands, so large and powerful. Who would have dreamed that the fingers could be so sensitive? They moved here and there, never anywhere for long, yet seeming to be everywhere at once.

'Let me turn over,' she demanded.

'When I'm ready.'

She thumped the pillow. *'Damn you!'*

He gave a rich laugh, observing lazily, 'That's been said to me before but never under these—precise—circumstances.'

She would have died rather than let him know how glad

she was to hear this. Instead she peered at him over her shoulder, with narrowed eyes. He understood her message, grinned and pulled back. Seizing her chance, Helena writhed over onto her back, grabbed him fiercely and pulled him over her. Now he came easily, sliding between her parted legs and thrusting deep inside.

She drove back against him fiercely, feeling her desperation explode in the fulfilment she found at last. She'd wanted this until she was half out of her mind, and that, of course, was what he'd meant to happen.

He'd won again and she didn't care, *she didn't care, SHE DIDN'T CARE!*

Let him win. Let him have everything as long as she could hold him inside her and feel that he was hers. While that was true she cared about nothing else.

Helena had half expected to find herself alone when she awoke, thinking that Salvatore would retreat from intimacy as soon as he had what he wanted. Yet he surprised her by being there, sitting on the bed, his eyes fixed on her, a thoughtful look on his face.

True, he looked away quickly, as though caught off guard, but she'd seen his expression before he could hide it, and she reached up her hand to touch his arm, making him look back.

'You're awake early,' he said. 'It's barely dawn.'

'Well, I can always go back to sleep,' she murmured in a sated, luxurious voice.

Smiling, he drew back the sheet, surveying her nakedness.

'If I let you,' he said.

The words might sound commanding but instinct told her otherwise. His desire for her was undiminished, just as she'd meant it to be. That meant the honours were even.

She saw him looking down on her with a half-smile and waited with beating heart for what he would say next.

But his cell-phone shrilled, smashing the atmosphere.

'Why didn't I think to turn it off?' he groaned, but added at once, 'Because you gave me something else to think of.'

They smiled at each other, but his smile faded as soon as he answered.

'What? But how can they—? I made it perfectly clear— To hell with them, I can't come now—' Then he groaned. 'All right, I suppose I'll have to—'

Helena slid off the bed and searched for her clothes. The magic time was over, but she had known it, against all the odds, and it would come again. That was enough for now.

When the call ended Salvatore was scowling.

'Damnation! I should have turned the phone off and left it off for days.'

'Days? Were we going to be here for days?' she enquired.

His scowl gave way to a wry smile. 'Who knows what might have happened?'

'Who knows indeed? But not now.'

'Now I have to get back to Venice and go to Switzerland for a meeting tonight. Some clown has made a mess of an important set of figures and if I don't sort it out it'll get worse.'

'Switzerland?' she echoed, halting her dressing in her dismay. 'For long?'

'Certainly a few days. Maybe a week. But think what evil-doings you can get up to when I'm gone. I'll probably return to find you've put me out of business.'

'Not at all,' she said at once. 'I fight fair. I'll wait until you return, *then* I'll put you out of business.'

He grinned and leaned over to drop a light kiss on her mouth. 'I'm really going to hate being away from you. Especially now.'

She nodded. There was no need for words. They understood each other.

In a few minutes they were in the motor boat, heading back across the lagoon. Gradually the Piazza San Marco came into view, the bells ringing from its distinctive tower, and as they neared Salvatore slowed down the boat.

'I'm in no hurry to get there,' he explained. 'Once we've landed we go back to being who we were.'

'But when you come back…' she ventured.

'Yes, when I come back there's a lot to be said. Until then—I'll just tell you this; you're the first person I've ever taken to the island.' His voice became deeper, quieter. 'And that makes me very glad. Do you understand?'

'Yes,' she murmured. 'I understand.'

'Then we understand each other,' he said, slipping an arm about her shoulders and drawing her close.

It wasn't a fierce or predatory kiss, but neither was it as gentle as the ones they'd exchanged on the island. He was telling her to remember how he could make her feel, how she could make him feel. He was telling her not to forget that he was coming back to claim her.

'Someone will see us,' she said, laughing through her delight.

'How? We're still out in the lagoon.'

But as if to prove him wrong a boat sped past so close that their own boat rocked with the waves, making them cling together.

'We'd better get home,' Salvatore said unsteadily.

He delivered her to the hotel, said a sedate goodbye and drove away without kissing her. Helena had expected nothing else. What was growing between them wasn't for the eyes of strangers.

It was the time of year when glass makers set out their new collections. Helena surveyed the new pieces that Larezzo had produced, and knew she could be proud. But what she could not do was rest on her laurels.

'We need a new oven,' she said, 'like the one Salvatore has.'

'It'll cost,' Emilio warned her.

'I know. I've posed for a few pictures but to raise that much I'm going to have to accept some serious assignments. But that will mean going back to England, at least for a while.'

'And you don't want to leave Venice,' Emilio said knowingly.

'I guess I don't,' she sighed. 'But neither do I want to give in. I'm still fighting him—in one way.'

'Even if not in another?' Emilio said, grinning.

'Well—just keep that to yourself. I'm not going to confuse the personal and professional.'

It was easy to say that now. What was between herself and Salvatore was something she couldn't name, but it brought her happiness, and it was easy to believe that things would work out somehow.

That was before she picked up the newspaper, and everything changed.

She stared a long time at the huge colour picture, trying to understand its meaning, but resisting it too because the real meaning was terrible.

The paper had gone to town featuring the new lines of the glass factories. Today it was Perroni's turn, and the spotlight was on a glass figure. It was beautiful, the most glorious piece Perroni had ever made, everyone said.

There was no detail, but the outlines were sculpted so skilfully that little was left to the imagination. The naked woman, created from glass that was almost clear but for a faint pearly tinge, stretched languorously back, her arms above her head so that the swell of her breasts was emphasised. Her face was featureless, but her hair flowed gloriously over her shoulders, and almost down to her waist.

Somehow the artist had caught her true nature, enticing,

fiercely sexual, outrageously tempting, knowing her own allure, enjoying it.

The photographer had taken her from several angles, and every picture was there in the newspaper. Underneath the headline read, *Helen of Troy.*

The paper had made the most of the story, strongly hinting that it was no coincidence that Salvatore's factory had produced this piece so closely following his association with the woman known as Helen of Troy.

> *The first Helen of Troy came down to us from history as the face that launched a thousand ships,*

the writer burbled.

> *And the people of Venice have recently seen this very thing for themselves at the Festa della Sensa.*
>
> *Advance orders for this daring work of art are said to top anything in Perroni's previous collections, meaning that the factory's fortunes are riding high again this year.*

Helena read the piece through several times in dead silence. Then she took a long breath.

'Fool!' she breathed at last. 'Is there a bigger fool in the world than me? So easy, so obvious, and I fell for it. All the time he's been laughing—jeering at me—'

Now she too was laughing, shaken with bitter mirth that grew more violent until her whole body ached.

At last she calmed down and made her way slowly to a chair by the window, overlooking the water. She almost collapsed into it as though the strength had drained from her, and leaned back, her face stony.

Certain things came back to her, things that had been

puzzling at the time but whose meaning was now brilliantly, horribly clear. Only the day before she'd bumped into Carla, apparently by chance, except that there'd been a mysterious significance in Carla's manner. While babbling innocently she'd studied Helena's face, as if searching for something. And her questions had been double-edged—did Helena know when Salvatore was returning to Venice? Had she heard about his line in glassware?

'She was trying to find out if I knew,' Helena mused. 'She must have known—everyone must have known—and they've been watching me to see the moment when I realised.'

This was what Salvatore had done to her; not only used her for profit, but also made her the laughing stock of Venice.

When she was sure she had herself under perfect control she returned to the newspaper and read the story through from the start. It was cleverly written, suggesting only that Salvatore had been romantically inspired by her. There was no hint of the cold-blooded calculation that actually lay behind it.

'They wouldn't dare,' she thought. 'They might think it, but only I will say it, because I know it's true.'

Cold-blooded. The words created a strange sensation in her, calling back the times when he'd been anything but cold, when the heat of his touch had inspired an even more fervent heat inside her, so that she had found a passion she'd never before known existed.

After years of being a figure of ice she'd discovered herself to be a deeply sexual woman, and all because a deceitful man had played her for a sucker. He'd warned her, but she'd refused to believe him, because at the same time something had been flowering in her that had nothing to do with the body, and everything to do with the heart.

Love. She hadn't dared give it a name but now it seemed to dance mockingly before her. The warmth and tenderness that had been growing in her, the moment when she had instinctively defended him to Carla, she'd thought this was love.

And all the time he'd been standing back, studying her to discover the best way to make use of her. Something caught in her throat when she remembered waking up to find him watching her, tenderly, as she'd thought; but actually calculating how much money he could make from putting her on the market.

How fiercely he'd seemed to worship her body! And all the time he'd been taking notes, for profit.

Antonio's photograph was looking at her from the bedside table, his face kind and cynical.

'You warned me what he was like,' she said. 'And I didn't listen. But those days are over.'

She rose to her feet, her expression grim.

'Now I know what to do.'

CHAPTER ELEVEN

THERE was another day to wait until Salvatore returned. He called her at once.

'I'd like us to meet immediately,' he said. 'There's something we need to talk about.'

'I agree. I'm on my way—'

'I'd rather—'

But the line was dead. Helena had hung up.

A brief, hurried walk brought her to the *palazzo*.

'Signor Veretti is in his study,' the maid said.

Salvatore opened his door as she approached and closed it behind them. The newspaper lay open on his desk.

'I know what you're thinking—' he began.

'If you really knew what I thought of you, you'd shrivel and die,' she informed him.

'I don't blame you for being angry. Since I saw that thing in the paper I've been trying to think how to explain to you—'

'But why bother? We both know how things stand. I'm really glad to have been useful to you.'

'Helena, I swear that piece was designed weeks ago, before I knew you.'

'Just an unfortunate coincidence! Please, Salvatore, don't insult my intelligence.'

Anger flashed in his eyes.

'I'm telling you the truth. You own a glass works yourself, you know how long these things take to produce.'

'I know I produced the devil's head in two days, and you also produced a head in two days.'

'Of course, it can be done in exceptional circumstances, but that was a one off. This—' he indicated the pictures in the paper '—was part of the line, created weeks before I met you. There's no connection.'

'And the name—Helen of Troy?'

'That didn't come from me. Some stupid journalist tacked it on, thinking he was being clever. After that everyone took it up. It was inevitable after we'd been seen together, but it wasn't my doing. It was just a malign trick of fate.'

'Malign? I don't think so. Since when were profits malign? It is true, isn't it, that this is outselling everything else?'

'Yes,' he said quietly. 'It's true. But I didn't arrange it that way. I ask you to believe me, Helena. *Please.*'

She gazed at him, wondering if she'd really heard him say please.

'I'm begging you,' he said quietly.

Suddenly she knew she was at a crossroads, seeing two directions. She could take the road of believing him, loving him, taking him on trust with the terrible risk of a betrayal that would destroy her. Or she could take the other direction, call him a liar to his face, walk away, safe forever from his machinations.

Safe and dead.

What had happened to her in his arms was a once-in-a-lifetime experience, offering joy as nothing else could ever do. If she left now she would never be hurt again, but there would be no joy, only a frozen desert. All she needed was the courage to take the risk.

'How can I believe you?' she asked in agony. 'You've always boasted that you'll stop at nothing to get the better of me, and you seem to have done so very thoroughly. If I believe in your innocence after this—well, you'll have got the better of me again, won't you?'

She faced him. He was very pale.

'You could think that,' he said slowly, 'or you could remember some of the things that—recently—well—we each remember what we want to.'

'I don't *want* to,' she cried. 'But I don't have any choice. You did this, it happened—'

'But other things happened too,' he said harshly. 'We both know that. Did they matter less?'

'I don't know. But I can't believe something just because I want to. Perhaps it's better to stick to what I can bear to remember. You said it wasn't safe to cross you, and I'd find that out. Well, I did, didn't I? And once a lesson is learned, it's learned. I can't unlearn it. I wish I could, but I can't.'

'Do you know what you're saying?' he said quietly.

'I'm saying that I understand what you've been trying to make me understand from the start. And I accept it. I don't want to, but I must.'

His eyes kindled.

'And when I tell you this was an unlucky accident—you won't even try to trust me?'

'No,' she said in a voice of defeat. 'I don't trust you. You've given me too many reasons not to.' She gave a sudden harsh laugh. 'Better to have it out in the open. Now we can stop deceiving each other. War to the death. So much simpler.'

'War to the death,' he agreed. 'Perhaps it was always inevitable. Gloves off, no holds barred.'

Something had changed in him. The gentleness that had briefly been there when he begged her now gave way to a look that his enemies would have recognised and feared.

Salvatore couldn't see how his face reflected the change.

He only knew that he had done for this woman what he'd done for no other. He'd said please. He'd even begged. It chilled him to remember that he'd begged, that she'd seen him do it and scorned him. If he could have wiped her from the face of the earth at that moment he would have done so.

'No holds barred,' she repeated. 'You talk of me trusting you, and there, in that picture, is the proof that you're lying.'

'Don't say that, I'm warning you—'

'Yes, you're *warning* me. How typical. You play the innocent but all the time you're making money out of me.'

'Only out of your body, which you've been doing yourself for years,' he said coldly.

'Because it's *mine!*'

'Ah, yes, of course,' he said in a tone of sneering discovery. 'I've infringed your copyright, haven't I? Your body is your property. It can be loaned or rented out for the evening, but the only one allowed to make money from it is you.'

'Exactly. And you can be sure that I'm going to do so. I'm going to take every offer, and believe me, there are plenty. Some of them go further than I've ever been before—'

'But they're the ones with the most cash attached,' he said with a derisive grin. 'Every garment removed has its price. You should certainly take every chance. I apologise for being so remiss about the fee. Here.'

He handed her a cheque he'd been scribbling.

'What's that?' she demanded, aghast.

'Royalties. After all, I've made use of your body without paying for it as your other clients do, so now we're even. I hope it's the correct amount.'

For a moment everything in the world was the colour of her agony. When the mist cleared she realised that she must have struck him. There was a livid weal across his face, just touching his mouth.

Then the murderous rage died as swiftly as it had flared,

and there was only the numbness of despair.

'I'll put this in the bank at once,' she said calmly. 'And, of course, I'll send you a proper invoice so that it can go through the books.' She gave him a brilliant smile. 'Just be careful which column you enter it in.'

'*Helena—*'

But she'd gone.

There was no time to think of Salvatore, even if she'd wanted to. The phone was never silent.

A fashion magazine sent an editor and several minions to Venice with instructions to search out a variety of locations to show off the large collection of clothes that arrived with them. Wearing a variety of bikinis she posed in gondolas and, as this was outside, a few passing tourists managed to take their own pictures, passing them on to the local newspaper, which printed them at once in glorious colour.

'She is quite shameless,' the *signora* observed, thrusting a newspaper out to Salvatore. 'Just look at her.'

'I would prefer not to,' he replied, pushing the paper aside. 'Her antics don't interest me.'

'Perhaps they should, since her name has been linked with yours. How could you have been so incautious as to let that happen?'

'Since she's Antonio's widow, there was no way to avoid it.'

'A widow! Oh, yes, she looks like a widow, flaunting herself, practically naked. Poor Antonio must be turning in his grave.'

'Not him,' Salvatore said with sudden wry humour. 'He would have loved this. Have you forgotten what he was like?'

'But he's dead.'

'Well, a man doesn't change his personality because he's dead.'

'*What did you say?*' she demanded, aghast.

'Nothing—I don't know what made me say that.' He shook his head as though trying to drive off a swarm of bees.

'I've no patience with that kind of fanciful nonsense, and nor did you used to have.'

'Antonio himself told her that he didn't want her to go around in widow's weeds.'

'You mean that's what she *says* he told her. How convenient that he isn't here to deny it!'

'He wouldn't deny it,' Salvatore said slowly. 'I can hear him saying it now. He always loved it when people envied the beauties on his arm.'

'Are you sure you aren't becoming like him?' the *signora* asked coldly.

'Quite sure,' Salvatore snapped.

'Then why have you let yourself be seen in her company? Admit it. You enjoyed flaunting her.'

Without warning he lost control of his thoughts. He was back again on the island, free to be open with her and to feel that she was open with him. Free from prying eyes: alone but not lonely, hidden from the world and glad to be so.

'People who think they know you, but actually they haven't the first idea.'

She'd said those words and they had found an echo in his heart, but who else would understand? Not one single person.

'You're mistaken,' he told his grandmother coldly. 'I had no such thought.'

'Nonsense, of course you did, but you never stopped to consider, did you? What does it do to this family's reputation to be connected with a woman who appears naked in public?'

'She was already connected with the family. And she isn't naked.'

'Isn't she? Look at that!'

The *signora* thrust the newspaper back under his eyes, so that he couldn't escape the picture of Helena leaning back

in a gondola. She was attired in a small black bikini, the twin
of the one she'd worn in the first picture Salvatore had ever
seen, the one he'd held in his hand only a few weeks ago,
swearing vengeance.

How long ago that seemed now. The first picture had been
relatively respectable, a woman on a beach with her husband.
The new picture was the reverse of respectable, showing
Helena stretched out luxuriously, her arms above her head,
her lips softly parted. This woman was wanton, created for
profitable sex.

And it was as false and wrong as his first view of her had
been. He knew her now, sensitive and vulnerable in ways he'd
tried and failed to understand.

In the matter of the figurine he was genuinely innocent.
Wrapped up in thoughts of her, he'd overlooked what was
happening in his factory, and failed to see the danger until too
late. Nor would there have been trouble if some over-clever
wit hadn't attached the title 'Helen of Troy' to a piece that
was otherwise anonymous.

Her anguished fury had left him stumbling for words and
he'd made everything worse. Clumsy oaf that he was, he'd
tossed money at her and seen the despair come into her eyes.
The memory still made him groan aloud.

His grandmother refused to give up the attack.

'That bikini covers almost nothing,' she snapped, jabbing
her finger at the picture. 'Look at her breasts, look at her—'

'That's enough!' Salvatore's voice crashed across her
words, shocking her to silence. He recovered himself quickly
and said in a strained voice, 'I see no need to discuss this
further. Please understand that the subject is closed.'

The cold finality in his voice made her wary. After a
moment she departed.

He seated himself and began to read a column of figures.
Nor did he look up as she swept out of the room, a rare dis-

courtesy that alerted her more than anything he'd said, or failed to say.

When he was safely alone Salvatore took back the newspaper and spread it out on the table before him, running his fingers over the picture as though he could bring back the vibrant living woman. But she was flat, dead. Certainly dead to him.

He began to tear the paper into small pieces and dropped them into the waste bin.

'Helena, my dear! What a pleasure bumping into you!'

Surprised, Helena looked up to see Salvatore's grandmother advancing towards her across the little café. Without waiting for an invitation she seated herself at Helena's table.

'Dear Helena, we're all absolutely agog to see that you've resumed your brilliant career.'

'I don't care for the career as such,' Helena replied. 'I'm putting the money in Larezzo, which is my life now.'

'Very wise. Of course, Salvatore is furious about it but that's all to the good if it shows him that he can't have his own way all the time. I really must congratulate you for the way you got his measure.'

'I think he and I sized each other up pretty accurately at the start,' Helena said carefully.

'So many women are fooled by him. He seems enchanted by them, but it's only a way of getting his revenge.'

'Revenge?' Helena echoed in disbelief. 'Don't tell me he's grieving for some girl who dumped him years ago. No, I don't believe that.'

'Quite right. Salvatore can deal with trivial romantic interludes. I'm talking about his parents.'

Now Helena was genuinely surprised. 'What about his parents?'

'His mother was my daughter, Lisetta. Guido, her husband,

treated her badly. They were in love at the start, but he got bored easily, and he had a wandering eye. Many wives in that situation cope by finding their own "distractions" but Lisetta couldn't. She loved him so much and he broke her heart again and again.'

Helena remembered the two pictures of Salvatore's mother, on her wedding day, when her face had blazed with joy, and then, just a few years later, a woman in despair, her face blank, so great was her agony and the need to hide it.

'Worst of all,' the *signora* continued, 'Guido used to bring his floozies home, and actually sleep with them there. There was a part of the building where his wife was forbidden to go. He said he wanted his "privacy".'

Helena flinched. This was a worse tale than she had expected.

'Lisetta died very suddenly. He married his then-current mistress, a good-time girl who bled him dry and almost brought him to ruin. He died about fifteen years ago, and Salvatore had to spend his whole youth working to repay his father's debts.

'Of course, he knew what was going on, even when he was a child, and it has affected his attitude to women. His mother is on a pedestal, but he despises what he calls "a certain kind of woman", and in his eyes practically all of them fall into that category.

'He amuses himself with them, but sooner or later they discover what he really thinks of them. You, of course, were never fooled.'

'No, I was never fooled,' Helena said slowly.

'I congratulate you on being so much smarter than the others.'

'You don't have to be very smart,' Helena said with a brittle laugh. 'Salvatore isn't subtle. I had my fun, now I'm going home to England.'

'Indeed? For long?'

'As long as it takes me to make the money I need.'

'When are you leaving?'

'Tomorrow afternoon.'

'Then I'll go and leave you to your packing. Goodbye, my dear, it's been *so* nice knowing you.'

Her plane was due to leave at three in the afternoon. Promptly at noon a young man came to her door to collect her luggage. When she'd finished paying her bill at the desk the young man was waiting to escort her to the motor launch. The back of the vessel was a cabin, lined with windows, and inside it she could see where her luggage had been placed. The driver, neatly dressed in uniform and cap, stood outside at the wheel. He didn't turn to acknowledge them, but Helena had a strange feeling that his back was familiar.

Her escort showed her into the cabin, said something to the driver, and left. The next moment the boat was pulling away from the hotel, gaining speed. Helena waited for the right turn which would take them in the direction of the airport, but instead they continued out into the lagoon.

'Hey!' She banged on the glass, trying to attract the driver's attention, but he didn't seem to hear.

She banged harder. This time the driver turned his head and looked at her.

It was Salvatore.

'No!' she screamed. *'Stop this boat.'*

But they went faster. From the direction it was clear that they were headed for the island, and if she let him take her there she would miss her plane.

'Salvatore!' she shouted, hammering harder on the glass. 'Don't you dare do this.'

He didn't even look round.

There was a door at the far end of the cabin. If she could

jump into the water, taking her bag with her tickets and passport, she could swim ashore.

But the door was mysteriously locked. She rattled it, but it was immovable. She was Salvatore's prisoner.

In a rage she ran to the other end of the cabin and hurled herself against the window.

'Salvatore! Let me out, do you hear?'

He ignored her.

She was being kidnapped and there was nothing she could do about it.

At last the island came into view. There was the cove where they had parked before, and he was heading for it again, reaching the little landing stage and tying up the boat, securing it with a chain.

The message was plain. Even if she managed to escape him she would never be able to use the boat to escape.

He unlocked the door at the rear and held it open, indicating for her to walk out.

'You must be mad to think you can get away with this,' she raged breathlessly.

'I don't see anyone who's going to stop me,' he replied in a casual tone that was even more infuriating than anger would have been. He sounded assured, even indifferent to her reactions and it made her want to kill him.

'What do you think you're going to gain?' she shouted.

'I'll stop you going to England. That'll do for a start. Are you going to get out of your own accord, or am I going to force you out?'

'Don't you dare touch me!'

'Don't be silly, of course I'll dare, and you know it.'

She did know it. There was no yielding in his face, no hint of the softer, more sensitive man she'd once thought she was discovering. There was only harshness, determination and a ruthless indifference to her feelings. He wouldn't balk at laying forceful hands on her.

While she was trying to calm her thoughts the answer came to her. She would pretend to give in, walk to the house with him, and as soon as she was alone she would make a call for help on her cell-phone.

'All right,' she said. 'Stand back and let me get out.'

'Apart from your handbag, just take one bag of clothes,' he said.

It would have been a pleasure to tell him what he could do with his orders, but she must fool him into thinking her docile, so she put the handbag under her arm and reached for a bag.

'Give it to me,' he said, taking it from her.

To her relief he seemed to accept her acquiescence without suspicion. Obviously he thought she was ready to yield easily. He would discover his mistake, she thought.

As before they walked up the sand and through the trees to the point where the whole of the tiny island lay before them. A few minutes brought them to the house.

'Come on, it's starting to rain,' he said, taking her arm.

They made it inside just as the heavens opened.

'You'll sleep in here,' he said, leading her into the main bedroom. 'I'll make some coffee and later we'll talk.'

'Whatever you say,' she agreed in what she hoped was an indifferent voice.

'Just one thing first,' he said. 'This.'

Before she knew what he meant to do he'd seized her handbag and whisked it away from her, opening it and taking out her cell-phone.

'*No!*' she cried, trying to grab it back, helplessly fighting with him, knowing it was useless.

Of course he hadn't been fooled for a moment. He'd waited until she was safely here before removing the phone, knowing there was nothing she could do about it.

'Give me that,' she demanded.

'And have you call the shore? I don't think so. I brought you here for a reason and you're going to stay until I say otherwise.'

'You've got a damned nerve, acting like a gaoler,' she raged. 'Get out of here now!'

'For the moment, I will. Don't even think of escaping.'

'Of course you can't let me get to England. How would you seize the factory then?'

'To hell with the factory,' he snapped. 'This is about you, about us. I'm not letting you go until we've sorted a lot of things out.'

'Don't give me that. I won't fall for it. This is just your way of fighting dirty. You knew that once I was back in England I could earn enough money to fend you off, so you took me prisoner, hoping I'll run out of cash and you can make me sell to you. Forget it. No matter how long you keep me here I'll get away in the end.'

He came close and spoke softly.

'Helena, you have no idea what you're up against. I'm not playing. This island is mine: my kingdom. My word is law. Nobody contradicts me.'

'You think I won't?' she challenged.

'On the contrary, I think you're foolish enough to try, but once you've discovered that there's nobody to help you, you're not foolish enough to try a second time. Go ahead, fight me. See where it gets you. Then come to your senses.'

'By coming to my senses you mean doing what you say.'

'Exactly. I'm glad you see it. It may save a lot of time.'

She barely heard the last words through a sudden crack of thunder. Now the rain was coming down hard. Salvatore looked up, frowning, and she seized her chance, shoving him aside strongly enough for him to fall on the bed, and making a run for it.

She was out in a moment, heading for the front door. Luck was with her. He hadn't locked it yet and she could wrench it open, fleeing out into the rain.

If she could get far enough away she could hide from him and when the weather calmed she could even swim for it. She was a strong swimmer and might stay afloat until a passing boat picked her up, but for the moment she could only run and run, propelled by anger more than fear. She wouldn't let him win—*she—would—not—*

The rain was pelting down, soaking her, turning the ground to mud, slowing her down. She could hear him just behind her and tried to run faster, but she was at the limit of her strength. She wasn't going to make it—but she must—she must—

It was too late. He had her, pulling her to the ground, holding her in a fierce grip. Now she could feel how fearsomely strong he was. There had never been any chance to escape him. She writhed uselessly but he held her without trouble until she stopped struggling and lay there gasping. Then he rose to his feet and began to walk back to the house, his arm fixed around her waist, forcing her to go with him. She tried to squirm free but she might as well not have bothered for all the notice he took.

Now they were at the house, he was locking the outer door and marching her into the bedroom, still holding her in a grip of steel. He didn't speak and there was something chilling about his silence as he dropped her down onto the bed and began to work on her buttons.

'No,' she gasped. 'You can't do this.'

'Yes, I can. From now on we do it my way.'

He wrenched open her jacket, tossing it aside, and with horror she realised that he meant to undress her forcibly. She lashed out but she could make no impact on him. One by one he removed her garments—blouse, trousers, pants, bra—until she was completely naked.

She lay there, looking up at him with hate. Memories of the passion they had shared flashed through her brain and she wanted to cry out her anguish that something so much like love should end this way, with a union that he clearly intended to force on her. After that there would be nothing left for her in the world.

He stood for a moment, looking down at her nakedness while his own chest rose and fell fiercely. Then he went into the connected bathroom, returning with a large towel that he tossed over her.

'Dry yourself,' he snapped. 'Do it quickly before you get pneumonia. I don't want your death on my conscience.'

He walked out.

CHAPTER TWELVE

THERE was a blinding light somewhere, insistently penetrating the darkness, calling on her to awaken.

She opened her eyes to find the sun streaming into her room, and Salvatore beside her.

'I brought you some tea,' he said briefly, setting it down and departing at once.

The tea was good and when she'd drunk it she felt better. The sleep, also, had helped. She hadn't expected to sleep at all, feeling sure that she would lie awake fretting, and at first it had seemed that she was right. Pictures and sensations flooded her brain, the sheer strength of him, holding her, stripping her, but then releasing her to spend the night alone. Then she'd seemed to sink into darkness.

Now she was awake. She could still feel his hands on her naked body, but whether the memory came from last night, or other nights when he'd held her in the fires of passion, she could not have said.

She looked down at herself, wearing a slip from the bag she'd brought with her, which contained only underclothes. Last night she'd dried herself hurriedly, put on the only clothes she could find, and huddled under the duvet. She looked around for the outer clothes he'd torn off her, but they had vanished.

He pushed the door open slowly. 'Are you ready for more tea?'

'I'd like my clothes back.'

'They're still wet; I've hung them up to dry.'

'I need something that covers me better than this,' she said firmly.

'All right.' He opened his buttons and removed his own shirt, handing it to her. 'I'm afraid this is all I have here at the moment. It will cover you completely.'

It did, buttoning up to the neck and enclosing her in warmth from his body. She regretted that at once. It was too intimate, as was the sudden view of him bare-chested. But he retreated at once, returning in a moment with more tea, and breakfast.

'Boiled eggs?' she queried.

'Don't you eat them? I thought all the English did.'

'As long as they're soft boiled.'

'If not I'll do them again. And don't look at me so suspiciously.'

'You think I shouldn't be suspicious after what you've done?'

'No, you probably should. But it's not for much longer. I want you to hear me out. After that I'll return your phone, you can call for help, accuse me of kidnap and by tonight I'll probably be in gaol. You can look forward to that, but listen first.'

'As though anyone at Venice is going to arrest you!' she said scornfully.

'What about the people on the other end? Wasn't someone meeting you at the airport? There'll be a hue and cry by now. Cross your fingers and you'll see me locked up yet.'

If she hadn't been so wary she might have thought his voice held a note of resignation, almost of defeat. But she suppressed the thought before it could flower. She'd let down her guard with him once. Never again.

'I look forward to seeing you locked up,' she said.

He looked at her for a moment, then left without speaking.

The eggs were perfect. She ate every last crumb then got out of bed and went for a wash. Putting back the shirt made her relatively decent, she reckoned.

Going through her bag, she found her things untouched except for the missing phone. There, in its own small compartment, was the glass heart Antonio had given her, and a sudden impulse made her put it on. It would tell Salvatore where her true heart lay, and it gave her a mysterious feeling of safety, as though Antonio was watching over her, as he'd often promised to do.

'Look him up in gaol,' she muttered. 'He doesn't mean it. He's just trying to get around me.'

But her own words didn't convince her. Once again she had the frustrating sense of thinking she knew all about Salvatore, only to find a new side to him that left her as confused as ever.

He was waiting on the terrace as she went out and sat a careful distance from him.

'What game are you playing?' she wanted to know.

'No game. You shouldn't be surprised that I stopped you returning to England, after your graphic description of what you were going to do when you got there. You knew what you were telling me—'

'That I could raise the money I needed to fight you—'

'Helena, let's be honest. Our fight has nothing to do with money or glass. We were made to belong together, but only if we could get other things out of the way first. We started as enemies but it didn't stop me wanting you more than I've ever wanted any woman. No—don't say it.' He held up a hand to silence her. 'Don't say anything about that figurine,' he continued. 'It was designed long before I met you, and its coming out now was an unlucky accident. It's just that…'

There he stopped, silenced by pain and confusion. Never in his life had he known how to describe his own feelings, or perhaps there simply hadn't been any worth describing. The few times he'd managed to find words he'd been talking by rote, saying what was proper, disconnected from meaning.

But now that the meaning overwhelmed him, burning him up with emotions more intense than any he'd allowed himself to feel before, he was struck dumb.

Clown! Idiot! Say something! Anything!

Why didn't she help him? She was the one who was clever with words.

'It's just that what?' she asked.

He made a helpless gesture. 'Nothing. You wouldn't believe me, anyway.'

The hope that had briefly flared in her died again.

'You're right, I probably wouldn't,' she sighed. 'Let's call it a day.'

She rose to go but he stopped her.

'Are you going to give up without even trying for what we might have?' he asked harshly.

'I'm not sure it's worth trying for. Won't we just be banging our heads against a brick wall? Let me go now.'

He'd taken hold of her, suddenly terrified at her ability to slip away from him in mind and heart if not in flesh. He grasped her body, knowing that her real self still eluded him but helpless to prevent it.

'I said let me go,' she gasped.

He did so, loosening his grip, but not quickly enough. As she pulled away there was the sound of a small crash and, looking down, they saw her glass heart in pieces on the ground.

'Oh, no!' Helena dropped to her knees.

'I'm sorry,' he said desperately. 'It was an accident, I didn't mean—'

She rose, clutching pieces of broken glass and backed away from him.

'Look what you've done,' she wept.

'Helena, please—we can get another one just like it.'

He knew he'd made a fatal mistake as soon as he uttered the words, and if he hadn't known her scorn would have told him.

'Just like it? How dare you? Nothing will ever be like it.'

'I know it was a gift from Antonio but—'

'You fool! It wasn't *a* gift, it was *the* gift, the first thing he ever gave me. I wore it when we married, and when he lay dying in my arms he touched it and smiled at me. Can you give that back to me?'

Dumbly he shook his head, feeling the ground shaking beneath his feet. He'd done a terrible thing and he didn't know how to put it right, or if there was any way to put it right at all. Her grief tore him apart and his own helplessness nearly drove him mad.

He was used to her strength but the agony of her sudden defeat almost destroyed him. And the sound of her tears brought back ghosts that had appalled him for years.

'Put it down,' he said, reaching out to her hands that were still clutching the broken glass. 'Put it down before you harm yourself.'

Somehow he managed to get it away without cutting her. She didn't try to move, just stood there shaking with misery.

'What is it?' he begged. 'For pity's sake, tell me.'

She shook her head, a gesture not of defiance but of helplessness.

'I'm not letting you go until you tell me everything,' he said in the gentlest voice Helena had ever heard him use.

But she couldn't respond. The brave face she'd worn since losing the only person in the world to whom she'd been close had suddenly cracked and fallen away, leaving her defenceless.

'Tell me about Antonio,' he said. 'We've never talked much about him, and perhaps we should.'

Still she couldn't speak through her sobs, and he just held her while the storm quietened.

'I know I was wrong,' he offered, 'but that's all I know. Helena, please…'

She choked and moved her head back a little, enough to speak.

'Antonio and I were never husband and wife in the proper sense,' she whispered, 'but in my own way I loved him. You wouldn't understand. You know nothing about love.'

'I might understand more than you know.'

'No, you see things so simply. You want, you get. Kindness and affection don't come into it.'

Salvatore groaned and dropped his head so that it just rested against her.

'I loved Antonio,' she said sadly, 'because he was gentle and generous, and he loved me without wanting to grab everything and drain me dry. That's what men do but he was different, better.'

'I don't understand. You could have had any man you wanted—'

'That's right, I could,' she said, recovering enough to speak defiantly. 'For the best part of sixteen years, I watched them slaver, pant, yearn. And I enjoyed it because I despised every one of them. I've been offered as much money as I liked if only I would—well, you can guess. But I never would. Never. Any man *I* wanted, yes! Only I didn't want any of them. They couldn't believe it. Of course they couldn't. No man ever does. They all thought the same as you, that I was anybody's as long as the money was right.'

'Don't!' he groaned. 'I've said I'm sorry about that. How can I make you believe it? I misjudged you. I've known for a long time. The first time we made love I knew you were different from what I'd thought.'

'You expected a prostitute,' she said bitterly.

'No, but I did expect a woman of experience. Instead—I can't say exactly—it was like making love to a girl. It might almost have been your first time.'

She was about to throw another bitter reply at him, but suddenly she noticed his eyes and realised there was something there she'd never seen before; not just earnestness, but a terrible honesty, as though his life depended on convincing her.

'It wasn't my first time,' she said in a gentler voice than she had meant to use. 'Just my first time in sixteen years.'

Once he would have been sceptical, but by now he had some hard-won wisdom. He urged her head against his shoulder, then stood there, wishing she would put her arms about him, or show some other sign of response.

'Look at me,' he whispered. 'Please, Helena, look up.'

Something in his voice seemed to affect her, and after a few moments she did as he asked, revealing a face so weary and vulnerable that he drew a shocked breath. The next moment he was kissing her, not with passion but softly, letting his lips linger for only a moment on her lips, her cheeks, her eyelids.

'It's all right,' he whispered. 'It's going to be all right. I'm here.'

Just why he expected this to reassure her he couldn't have explained. She didn't want him here. She wanted him consigned to the devil; she'd made that plain enough.

'Helena—Helena…'

She made the tiniest possible movement towards him with her hand, and he thought, but couldn't be sure, that she murmured his name. He didn't wait for more but lifted her carefully and took her back into the bedroom, laying her down on the bed and stretching out beside her.

'Trust me,' he said.

He drew her close to him again, not making love, but offering warmth and security, and she seemed to understand at once because she clung to him with a helpless need he'd never known in her before, even at the height of her desire. He had no defence against the sensation which took him by surprise, upsetting every preconception, triggering feelings that alarmed yet exhilarated him.

'What happened?' he asked at last.

'When I was sixteen I met a man called Miles Draker. He was a fashion photographer and he said he could make me a big name. I fell totally in love with him. I'd have done anything he wanted. I didn't care about being famous, I just wanted to be with him all the time.

'It was a wonderful life, making love at night, taking pictures by day. While he trained the camera on me he used to say things like, "Remember what we did last night—think that it's happening now—now imagine you're trying to please me." And I did. Then I'd look at the pictures afterwards and see it in my own face. I thought it was my love that showed, but of course love wasn't what he wanted. Pretty soon I was a success, just the way he had said. He gave me a contract, tying me to him, and I was the happiest girl in the world.

'And then, just when we were starting to hit the big time, I discovered I was pregnant. I was so thrilled.' She gave a soft mirthless laugh. 'When I look back I can hardly believe how delighted I was. Fool! Idiot!'

'Don't call yourself names,' he said.

'Why not? They're all true.' Her voice took on a tortured edge as she went on, 'Stupid, ignorant cow, brainless—'

'Is that what he called you?' asked Salvatore, who was beginning to discern the horrible end of this story.

'That and a dozen other things. I thought he'd be pleased but he was furious. Just when we were getting somewhere I was going to "mess it up". He wanted me to get rid of the baby and when I wouldn't he screamed at me.' Her voice rose almost to a shriek and she began to thump him, crying, 'Thoughtless, selfish bitch—'

'I said stop,' he told her, covering her mouth with his own.

She was shaking violently and at first she continued

thump him, although with no strength behind it. He simply countered the blows by holding her steady until she gave up and yielded, her lips moving softly in what might have been a kiss, if only he could be sure.

'Go on,' he said at last. 'What did he do?'

'He kept on and on at me, saying it was his big chance as well as mine, and how could I be so selfish? But I couldn't do it. This was *my* child, depending on me for protection. I tried to make him understand but he just got angrier.

'I remember him sneering, "You weren't actually thinking of marriage, were you?"'

'Were you?'

'I might have been once, I can hardly remember. If so I abandoned the idea pretty fast. He was so determined to "get rid of the problem" as he put it that he turned into a monster.'

'Did he hit you?' Salvatore demanded in mounting outrage.

'No, of course not. He might have left a mark and that would have damaged the merchandise. He had his own methods. Once he brought a "medical advisor" to talk to me. When that didn't work he just nagged, going on and on and on, screaming, shouting, calling me names all the time we were working.'

'Why didn't you just walk out?'

'He had me tied to a contract. Besides, I knew I'd have to leave as soon as I started to show. I just wanted to earn while I could, so that there'd be something to live on. If that meant putting up with his nastiness, it was worth it. But then—' she shuddered '—then…'

'Go on,' he said gently against her forehead.

'One day when he was really bad I started crying, and I couldn't stop. The next thing I knew, I'd lost the baby.'

'Maria vergine!' Salvatore muttered.

'After that he thought everything was going to be fine.

He'd got what he wanted, and what else mattered? When I wouldn't go back to him he threatened me with legal action. But then a magazine gave me a big spread. Suddenly I was in demand as never before. I got taken on by an agency who told me to leave everything to them.'

'What did they do?'

'I never asked; I only know they managed to tear up the contract. I got a phone call from Draker, screaming abuse at me, but I hung up halfway through, and never heard from him again. A few years later I saw him taking seaside photographs of tourists. He didn't see me.

'After that I concentrated on my career and nothing else. And it took off. I had more work than I could cope with. There were always men who wanted to be seen with me, so I let them, but they never got anything else. I was dead inside and all I could feel for them was contempt. Until I met you I hadn't slept with a man for years, nor wanted to.'

Salvatore held her in silence, but inwardly he was groaning. He wanted to beg her to stop because he couldn't stand any more of such a nightmarish story. But in his heart he knew that the real nightmare was the way he'd lined himself up with all the others.

He was as bad as any of them; no, worse, for he'd always sensed something wrong. Instinct had told him from the first that she didn't quite fit his image of the rapacious harlot, yet he'd blinded himself to whatever didn't suit him. As her power over him had grown so had his anger at her for possessing such power. When he'd felt his heart touched he'd moved fast to shut it down.

'And then there was Antonio,' Helena said. 'He was facing the end of his life alone, and all he asked of me was to be with him. He knew I had money of my own because he'd safeguarded it for me, so he never thought I was marrying his wealth.'

'Don't,' Salvatore groaned.

'No, I wasn't aiming that at you. I'm just saying that he knew he could trust me, and that helped our whole relationship. I started out being fond of him, and we grew closer and closer. It was me he wanted—not my body, *me!* He was the only man I could ever say that about.'

Not any longer, he thought, but uncharacteristically lacked the confidence to say it.

'He took such wonderful care of me,' she mused.

'You should have told me long ago,' he murmured. 'But then, I didn't ask, did I? I never said one word that might have encouraged you to open yourself up to me as a person. I only thought about how madly I wanted you, and how you were leading me a merry dance.'

'I meant to,' she said. 'After that first day I was so angry at the way you instinctively thought the worst of me. It never crossed your mind that I might have been sincerely fond of Antonio. I soon discovered that you knew nothing about love because you don't believe in it.'

Suddenly she moved away slightly and turned, propping herself up on one elbow and surveying his face. 'Shall I tell you something that'll really annoy you?'

'Anything that gives you pleasure,' he said wryly.

'I came to Venice with the fixed intention of selling you Larezzo. Antonio had told me that you'd probably make an offer and he was glad because it would give me some more financial security.'

She stopped, for Salvatore had covered his eyes and groaned.

'And I drove you into opposing me by the way I behaved,' he said at last. 'I'm to blame for everything.'

'No.' She stroked his hair. 'After what your grandmother told me I guess a lot of it was inevitable.'

He stared. 'What did she tell you?'

'About your father, and how he broke your mother's heart with his other women.'

After a moment Salvatore asked quietly, 'Is that all she told you?'

'Only that your mother died suddenly.'

He sighed. 'There's a bit more to it than that.'

When he fell silent she moved closer and touched his face gently. 'Do you want to tell me?'

'Did my grandmother say that he brought his women home, and that they lived with us in a special part of the house where none of us were supposed to go?'

'Yes, she said that.'

'My mother encountered them sometimes. Then she'd retreat to her room and I'd hear her weeping. If I tried the door it was always locked. I wanted to comfort her, but she wouldn't let me. I know now that there was no comfort anyone could have given her.

'There was one woman whom my mother saw often because she wandered through the house whenever she wanted. She did it deliberately, I have no doubt of that. She wanted to be seen. She was letting everyone know that she considered herself the future mistress of the house, and my mother understood that message.

'Then one night I stood outside her room, listening for her weeping, but it didn't come. She never made a sound again. She'd taken her own life.

'Since then I've always wondered, if I'd been more suspicious of the silence, if I'd forced the door open, would I have been in time to save her? I'll never know.'

She was too shocked to utter comforting words where no comfort was possible. She only held him tight, stroking his head as tenderly as a mother with a child, and neither spoke for a long time.

'How old were you when that happened?' she whispered at last.

'Fifteen.'

'Sweet heaven!'

'I grew up hating the idea of love because I'd seen what it could do. All women except my mother were monsters. It was safer to believe that. I resented you because you gave me thoughts I was ashamed of. I wanted you so badly that I'd forget everything else. All the things that had seemed important before were pushed aside, including my responsibilities to other people. In other words, I started acting like my father. I hated myself for that, and I almost hated you. But that was then. Not now.'

'And now?' she asked, breathless with hope.

'Now I can say to you what I swear I've never said to any other woman: I love you. I thought I'd never say those words because I was sure they'd never mean anything to me. And I was content with that. I didn't *want* to know. The world was safer without love. *I* was safer, and now I think I've always been seeking that safety, ever since the night I stood outside my mother's silent room, and the world disintegrated.'

She almost said, 'Safety—you?' The mere thought of this powerful man knowing fear and uncertainty was incongruous. But she understood him now. He'd allowed her to see through the armour he wore against the rest of the world, into the wilderness, the place where that shattered fifteen-year-old boy still lived, cowering, begging for it not to be true.

She tightened her arms lovingly about him.

'I didn't see it then,' he continued, 'but I see it now. With you I found another world, one where there was love but no safety, and I think that's why I was against you from the start.'

He gave a wry, self-mocking smile as he said, 'I was afraid. That's another thing I've never said before, but I can say it now. You were the unknown, and I didn't have the courage to face it, until you took my hand and showed me the way. I can't promise you an easy love, because it's so new to me that

I'm clumsy and ignorant. But I can promise you a faithful love, for all my life, and yours.'

She couldn't speak. Tears stung her eyes.

'And if you can't love me in return,' he said huskily, 'then—' a tremor went through him '—then I guess I'll just have to be patient and persuade you slowly.'

'No need,' she assured him. 'You and I have played games about this from the start, but the time for games is over. I love you—and I'll always love you, through good times and bad. And there will be bad times, I know that. But they'll pass as long as we have each other.'

He nodded, stroking her face gently, whispering, 'How can you possibly love me?'

'I can't imagine. It defies explanation, but the best things usually do.'

'After all I've done, I wouldn't blame you if you hated me.'

'Let me show you,' she said.

This loving was different from all others, slow and gentle, their eyes meeting constantly, but also their hearts and minds. With tender gestures she reassured him, reaching out to the heart that he'd revealed to her and to nobody else in the world.

She knew that if she betrayed his trust she would destroy him. From now on his fate was in her hands and she would defend him with all the strength of her love.

Love. For the first time the word did not sound strange.

Salvatore awoke to find himself in darkness and her gone from his arms. For a moment he wanted to cry out with desolation, but then he saw her standing naked at the window, looking out over the lagoon, to where Venice could just be seen in the distance. So near, and so far.

'I thought you'd gone away from me,' he murmured, coming up behind her, and nuzzling her neck. 'You could have made that phone call.'

'I did. I found my phone and called my friends in England

to say that I missed the plane but there was nothing to worry about. I'll have to go over for a week to fulfil my contract, but I'll be back soon.'

'With a fortune to spend on Larezzo?'

'That's right.'

'Since we're talking business, I have a proposition for you. I'll make you an interest-free loan, then you'll have all the cash you need to invest.'

'Interest-free, huh? And what do you get in return?'

'You—as my wife. Then I can keep an eye on what sharp practices you're up to.'

'But of course. No business deal can succeed without a binding contract.'

'It's a pleasure to find a woman who understands business.'

'You realise that where that's concerned I'll still fight you?' she said.

'I'd expect nothing else.'

'No holds barred.'

'Exactly,' he agreed. 'And let's be frank, it won't just be business where no holds are barred. This isn't going to be a peaceful marriage.'

'So I should hope.'

For a long time after that they didn't move, but stood contentedly leaning against each other.

Strangely the thought of Antonio came to her now. Or perhaps it wasn't so strange, for he'd promised to take care of her, and by throwing her together with Salvatore he'd done it very thoroughly.

Not that he could have known this would happen. Of course he couldn't.

But somewhere in the distance she imagined she could hear his laughter, and his kindly, mocking voice saying, 'Fooled you, *cara.*'

And when she looked across the lagoon the sun was just breaking out, heralding the glorious new day.

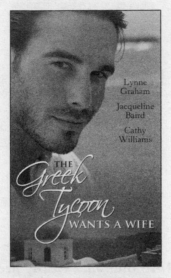